MOONLIGHT BECOMES YOU

LUCKY MOON BOOK ONE

M.J. O'SHEA
PIPER VAUGHN

To all the Lucky Moon fans out there. The boys are back, new and improved. Thanks for the love and support over the years. — Piper and MJ <3

CHAPTER ONE

Now…
London

SEX AND ALCOHOL HUNG HEAVY IN THE AIR. HE couldn't seem to get rid of the smell. It was cloying. Nauseating. He wanted to scrub it from every surface until all that was left was *clean*. Shane had never thought the life would get old—endless sex, drugs, and rock 'n' roll. But it had. It was. Old. Or maybe it was just him. Old before he was even thirty-two.

Shane rolled onto his side and punched one of the many pillows that surrounded him, then drew it to his chest and burrowed deeper under the covers. A couple of hours of sleep, that was all he asked. He'd sent the groupies from his room over an hour ago. But no matter what position he tried, he couldn't seem to get comfortable.

Closing his eyes, Shane forced himself to concentrate on breathing. Nice and slow. In and out. One breath. Two. Then another. A fourth. A fifth. A dozen. Gradually, his muscles loosened, his body grew lax, and he started to drift off. The last thing he remembered before sleep claimed him was a name.

Jesse....

Then....
Chicago

SHANE VENTURA SAT in the library of his soon-to-be ex-high school for the very first time, fiddling with a blue pen in his hand. He stared at the carpet and thought about how much better that institutional stretch of puke green would look if he could just get at it with his pen and draw some dope designs into the fibers. The ugly-ass carpet blurred as he let his eyes fall out of focus. If he wasn't careful, he'd end up falling asleep.

He couldn't believe he was stuck in the library while his brother and their friend Dre were at the skate park, probably picking up a fat sack to smoke later. Those bitches better not start without him. He'd bagged groceries at the supermarket for a week, loading bags into cars in the freezing-fucking-cold Illinois winter for a third of that weed. If they smoked his share, he was going to kick some ass.

Shane toyed with the zipper on his hoodie, ignoring the glares from the table of preppy girls next to him. When one of them turned to stare a second time, he glared right back and zipped it again, making the longest, slowest sound possible. The girl huffed and turned around. Shane chuckled, then looked up at the clock.

Two fifty.

Whatever nerd-alert they'd hired to tutor him had exactly one minute before he was going to book. Yeah, the counselor's office said three, but he didn't give a shit. Didn't give a shit about high school either. He just didn't want to be a dropout loser five months before he could get out legally, didn't want his little brother Nick to get the idea that ditching school permanently was a good plan. Still, he wasn't going to sit around forever and wait. Shane looked at the clock again.

Two fifty-one. *That's it.*

Shane shuffled his stuff together and got ready to bounce. He'd stop by the office and tell them his tutor didn't show. Then he was free to do whatever the fuck he wanted. He had put in the effort. The guidance counselors could kiss his ass. He was standing up to go when the library door creaked open and some kid wandered in with a stack of books the size of Lake Michigan. *Shit.* Nerd for Hire had shown up.

"A-are you Shane Ventura?"

A pudgy, pale white face emerged from behind that teetering pile of books. The white moon of a face was surrounded by dark-brown hair in what had to be the worst bowl cut Shane had ever seen. He had glasses, braces, a big honker of a nose—Jesus, it was the whole nine yards. The only thing missing was headgear, and he probably wore that at night.

Seriously, this kid's parents must have it in for him.

The face and that disaster of a haircut were followed by a soft body covered in a navy blue polo shirt—of all dumb-ass things—and khakis that were pleated, pulled up practically under his fucking armpits, and belted, for shit's sake. *Belted.* The only thing he was missing was a pair of.... No, never mind. There they were. Fucking penny loafers. The kid looked like Shane's grandpa Ralph.

Where the hell did they find this loser? I'll eat him for an after-school snack.

"I s'pose I am Shane Ventura. You are?"

"J-Jesse. Seider. I'm here to help you with Algebra II and chemistry."

"What are you, an eighth grader?" Shane looked the kid up and down, hoping to intimidate him into submission.

"No, I'm a j-junior. Are you ready t-to start?"

"Yeah. Let's make it quick. Got a fat bowl waiting for me at home."

Dorky Pants looked at him unwaveringly, his face much more confident than that shaky little voice. Shane didn't care. The kid only came up to his chin. Shane could easily flatten the butterball if he wanted to.

"I'm not going to pretend I know what that means. B-but you have an hour with me th-three times a week. It's in the contract you signed."

"Why the hell do you care if we really do this? Just sign off on my paper here, and let's hit the road."

"I w-won't get my tutoring credit for the college applications unless your grades and test scores improve."

"That's what this is about for you? College?"

"D-did you think I was doing it for fun? S-sit. We're getting through your math homework if nothing else."

Shane looked the kid over. There was a surprising amount of steel in those gray eyes, practically hidden by his Bill-Gates-circa-1982 glasses, but there all the same. Shane snorted and shrugged. It wasn't like he had much of a choice.

"Fine. Might as well. Pull your pants out of your ass crack, and let's get started."

WHAT A DICK. Jesse had been raised to think the best of most people. His mom expected him to be a nice guy. But it was really freaking hard when there were people like Shane in the world, who seemed to exist only to make his life a pain in the ass. He just wanted some volunteer credits—not get hassled to the end of his patience. Yeah, the guy was super hot, with creamy, pale golden skin; a dark fall of hair; heavy, curly eyelashes; and big old heartbreaker eyes. The works. Too bad pretty didn't come on the inside too.

"Turn to page fifty in your textbook. We have to get this assignment done first. It was due three weeks ago." Jesse tried to sound unintimidated. He wasn't intimidated. He was annoyed. Yes, annoyed.

"Do we have to start with math? I didn't get this dumb shit three weeks ago, so I didn't do it. Why do you think I'm gonna do it now?" Shane stared sullenly at the avocado-green Formica on the library table and didn't make a move to open his book.

Jackass. "Because I'm going to explain it to you. I'm a tutor. That's what tutors do."

Shane whistled loudly and banged his palm on the table. The librarian glared at him. "We've got a sassy one, folks."

"You're s-so annoying."

"Watch your mouth, mathlete. I don't just keep pencils in my pockets."

Jesse had been acting so brave—acting being the key word. But the second Shane Ventura, resident badass, even vaguely threatened him, he felt like shuddering into the floor. Bravado gone.

Don't be such a sissy. You need these credits, and they assigned him to you.

Jesse couldn't wait to get out of there. He tried not to think about how he had to come back two more times that week and three times a week for the rest of the school year. *Tutoring credits, my ass. I'll deserve some sort of presidential commendation if I make it out alive.*

"F-fine. Just open your book and we'll try to get this over with."

Shane rolled his eyes, like Jesse might not have already gotten that he was annoyed and didn't want to be there. You know, just in case.

"Fine," he said.

At least he actually opened his damn book. Good. Time to get to work.

An hour later Shane looked up from the problem he'd just completed. "I think I get it." And he did. It was probably the first time he understood what was going on in math since junior high. First time someone ever bothered to really show him too.

Jesse scribbled down another similar problem on his paper. "Here, do this one without my help."

Shane started working through the complex problem, and just like the last one, he was actually *getting* it. An hour ago, he'd have balled up the paper and thrown it in the nearest trash can on his way out the door. Jesse watched him intently as he completed the problem. Shane got hung up for a second, but Jesse waited patiently for him to finish without giving him any hints. Then Jesse looked over Shane's work and nodded.

"You got it. We'll go over these again on Wednesday, but I think it's in your head pretty well."

Shane looked at Jesse in surprise. "Hey, what happened to the stutter?" He'd been so intent on figuring out his work after he stopped dragging his feet that he hadn't noticed the change in Jesse's demeanor.

"Oh, I, uh, only do that when I'm nervous. Uncomfortable, you know? Not usually."

Shane chuckled. "I made you nervous?"

"No. You scared the shit out of me. Totally different."

"Wow. Perfect prissy boy swears."

Jesse just shook his head. "You don't know me, Shane. Do me the favor of not jumping to conclusions. I didn't do it to you."

Shane thought for a second. The kid was right. He hadn't treated Shane like all the teachers did—like a punk, and they were just waiting for him to fail so they could get rid of him. Maybe he *was* a punk, but it was nice for a minute to be treated with respect.

"Fair enough." He gathered his stuff together and stood.

"See you Wednesday?" Jesse looked a bit uncertain after his big speech. Shane decided to let the kid off the hook instead of messing with him.

"Yeah. See you Wednesday."

He turned and swaggered out of the library, knowing every kid was watching him, hoping he'd do something they could whisper about. So he slammed the swinging library door open as hard as he could and chuckled when it crashed against the wall and a few books fell off the shelf. *There. Talk about that, bitches.*

Now....
London

SHANE OPENED HIS EYES, surprised that for once, whatever hotel room he'd woken up in was relatively clean and undisturbed. His usual mornings weren't complete without sheets strewn all over the floor among empty liquor bottles and bags of the previous night's entertainment. But today, his vision wasn't blurred by the perpetual hangover that usually accompanied the alcohol, and his head was remarkably free of weed haze, and—oh shit... was he *sober?* And alone. How refreshing. Maybe it was a good habit to get into, kicking the twinks out before they got comfortable. And they took most of their mess with them. Good. It wasn't like he wanted them there in the first place.

He pushed away disturbing memories of the night before, or rather the non-night. He didn't want to dwell on how he couldn't seem to care enough to drink or do lines with his little groupie party or stick his dick anywhere but into a pair of sleep pants. He'd gone to bed sober for the first time in years, ignoring the sex going on around him, miserable as always. And that was exactly how he felt when he woke up.

Miserable.

No matter how shitty he felt, Shane had to get his game face on. His band, Luck, was set to meet with Moonlight and their lead singer, the great Kayden Berlin, in a little over an hour. They were on Berlin's turf, too, and about to spend a lot of time living very close together as they toured all spring and summer. Shane hoped the guy wasn't an asshole or some super-straightedge prick who'd look down on a little bit of rock 'n' roll fun. Shane tried to ignore the fact that it hadn't been fun for him in years. Maybe not even at the beginning.

That's because your life is empty.

He could hear Jesse's voice in his head and tried to push it away. His life was empty—or full, rather. Full of the wrong things: too many drugs, too much alcohol, too many nameless one-night stands. It was the stuff of rock-star fantasies, what every kid wanted when he dreamed of fame.

It was expected of him. It was the last fucking thing he wanted. It hadn't taken Shane very long to figure out that the lifestyle wasn't him. By then it was too late. Jesse was gone.

Shane forced himself into the shower in an effort to make himself presentable. This meeting with Moonlight had to go well. *Something* had to go well.

He scrubbed down quickly, dried off, and chose his clothes with care to give the exact right impression. He pulled on a pair of artfully ripped Dior skinnies—expensive but still with an air of "I don't give a fuck"—a thin white T-shirt, and a charcoal vest with a faint pinstripe. He left the vest hanging open. Didn't want to look like he was trying too hard.

Two chains were sitting in a shallow bowl in the bathroom. He draped both over his neck like he did every day. One had the band's stylized four-leaf clover logo dangling from it and was worn front and center, right where everyone could see it. The other hung underneath it, smaller and far less noticeable. It was a simple little silver shamrock, bought for him years ago when Luck was still playing in his dad's basement for fun.

It wasn't something he needed or wanted anyone to notice, but he'd have felt naked without it. That necklace was the only thing he owned that meant a damn thing to him.

After surveying his look with a shrug, Shane finished by shoving a fedora over his damp black hair. He lined his blue eyes in their customary charcoal. The eyeliner hid the fact that he hadn't slept well in months. Sort of. He could still see dark circles in the harsh fluorescent light of the bathroom mirror, stark even against his naturally tan skin.

Fuck it. Heroin chic, right?

He tried not to linger on the fact that the fucked-up Cobain was the rock idol he chose to channel. He'd never set out to be such a colossal fuckup. He had to get his shit together and fast. Maybe this tour was a chance for change.

Shane laced up his boots and left the room, then walked four doors down the hallway to meet in Nick's suite for a pre-Moonlight conference with his band.

"Dude, I'm so fucking pumped!"

Nick's enthusiasm was hard to resist, but Shane couldn't help giving him some shit.

"Fuck, Nicky, you're about one squeal away from obnoxious fangirl. Am I gonna have to leave you up here when we go meet the band?"

"Shut up, homo. I can admire brilliance in another artist. I mean, those piano solos are epic, and I wanna fuckin' *marry* the guitar riff in 'Black Heart.' That thing gives me wood every time I hear it. And his *voice*."

Shane tried to control his snort. "Hey, maybe you can get Berlin to play you a little private show. Then you two can hold hands and, like, waltz into the sunset and shit."

Nick scoffed. "In your dreams, bro. I'm never going to be a full-time cast member of the 'mo show like you. I might have an appetizer here and there, but boy love will *never* be my main course."

"Yeah, he likes the sushi too much!" Dre, their drummer, chuckled at his own joke.

Nick made a dramatic air-guitar motion and crowed

"Wasabiiiii" at the top of his lungs. Dre and Nick collapsed into laughter and fist-bumped over their mutual love of the sushi. Shane felt vaguely nauseated. "Are you two fuckers high?"

They both pulled their most innocent faces. "Nah, dude. We're cool," Dre muttered, looking at the ground.

Shane wondered when he'd become the dad of the group. "*Fuck.* Just don't act like assholes, okay? All right, we're done here. Any last and final words before we go down to meet our masters?"

Nick raised his hand like he was going to say something but made a loud farting noise with his armpit instead. Shane sighed, feeling like the three years between him and his brother were more like a hundred.

"That was brilliant, Nicky. Thank you for your contribution." Shane looked at the others, who remained silent. "I guess that means we're going. Let's get this show on the road. I've got a fifth of Cîroc waiting for me back at the room."

Shane was nervous. *Nervous,* for Christ's sake. He couldn't remember the last time he had butterflies in his stomach over anything, let alone simply meeting another band. But it wasn't the band Shane was worried about. It was Berlin. Even more specifically, it was his eyes.

Shane had seen those eyes on TV hundreds of times. Sea green and piercing, they made Shane uncomfortable, but he could never be sure if it was a good uncomfortable or bad. That morning, he was leaning toward bad. He was worried about meeting Berlin, for sure, and found himself wishing he was anywhere else.

Don't be a fucking idiot. Why are you letting this guy get to you? Luck's been around nearly twice as long as these losers.

The pep talk didn't help. Neither did insulting Moonlight in his head. Shane tried to push it down and focus on Nick's jubilance instead. Even Dre and Will were vibrating, excited to meet the genius in the next room. Shane squeezed at his temples with his thumb and forefinger. *Fuck.* Here goes nothing. He put on his best "don't give a shit" face, took a deep breath, and opened the door to their posh London hotel's conference room.

The room was filled with people: musicians, managers, agents, caterers, lighting and tech guys, and scattered around with cameras were a few privileged members of the press.

Shane didn't see any of them.

It was like one of those cheesy scenes in a movie when the whole crowd blurs into insignificance and that one perfect person sticks out, illuminated by fate or kismet or the gods shining down. In this case it was a well-placed halogen, shining off a crown of icy-blond hair and a gorgeous face chiseled out of pale, pale skin. Shane shivered, unable to control his instantaneous reaction to the man across the room. It was him. It had to be.

Kayden Berlin.

He stood in the corner, not hiding but rather presiding over the room from what could easily have been his throne, if he were seated. People swarmed around him, all vying for a moment of his attention. He surveyed the room with mild interest. Those glaringly bright sea-green eyes never landed for more than a few seconds on any one object. Until he saw Shane. Then he stared for long, intense moments until Shane's line of sight was broken by the fiery little ball of energy that was Emmanuel Cortez, Luck's manager.

Em might have looked like fluff, and Shane's considerable height practically dwarfed him, but he was a force to be reckoned with. He'd managed to keep Nicky mostly in line for years. Despite their dubious first impression of him, he earned their respect, and they all trusted him implicitly.

"Hi, guys. I'm glad you made it. Come meet the boys from Moonlight!"

Shane nearly laughed at his excitement. "Em, you're supposed to be our manager, not the president of the Kayden Berlin fan club."

Em placed a hand on his expensively clad hip. "I *am* a fan of Moonlight's music, thank you very much."

Shane waited silently, knowing their manager could never keep anything in for very long. He wasn't disappointed.

"What? Okay, so Kayden's a total sweetie pie, and the man is beautiful. Don't tell me you haven't noticed, Shane. I know you too well."

Shane gave Em a knowing wink. "Let's go meet the foreign prince and get this dog-and-pony show over with."

The butterflies started again as soon as Shane got close to Kayden Berlin. Even stripped of the glam and glitter of the stage, the man had a presence that seemed to... *glow*. And then he smiled, and Shane's gut dropped to his toes. His smile was, in a word, stunning.

Kayden greeted Em. "Hi, doll." His voice was a soft tenor—warm, rich, and lightly accented. It startled Shane for a moment. The British accent couldn't be heard in Kayden's singing, as was typical with foreign bands. Shane hadn't thought about how Kayden's speaking voice would be different.

"Hi, sweetie," Em trilled back. He stood on his tiptoes to kiss Berlin's cheek.

Since when was Em in kissing mode with strangers he just met?

"Kayden, these are the boys from Luck. We have the Ventura brothers, Shane and Nick. This is Andres, better known as Dre, and last but not least, we have William Paige. Will plays the keyboards. You'll have to give him some tips sometime."

Will looked like he was about to murder Em. Talk about having your balls ground up and served on toast. Poor guy had basically just been signed up for a freaking piano lesson with Berlin. Pride totally gone on that one. Shane winced.

Berlin had a smile and a handshake for Dre, who'd worked his way to the front of the group. He smiled and shook hands with Will, too, who also got a small apologetic shrug. It wasn't until he got to Nick that his demeanor changed completely.

"Nick Ventura, your reputation precedes you." With the crisp accent, it was hard to tell how insulting Berlin meant to be. The open friendliness from only moments before was gone, however. Nick seemed unperturbed.

Can't he feel the ice coming his direction? Shane, for one, was confused. What did Berlin have against his brother?

"Dude, I'm so pumped to meet you. That guitar riff on 'Black Heart' is seriously legendary. I'd love to just sit down and jam with you sometime."

"Perhaps," Berlin answered, not outright rudely but nowhere near friendly. Nick finally noticed the chilly reception he was getting and stepped back, clearly taken by surprise.

Shane extended his hand, hoping to defuse the sudden awkwardness. "Shane Ventura. This tattooed monkey is my younger brother."

"I know who you are," Kayden replied, his demeanor as icy as it had been with Nick, if not more so. His eyes flicked over Shane's hand, but he didn't reach out to take it.

"Oh." Shane dropped his arm back to his side, unable to think of anything else to say. He had a few inches on the other singer, but Kayden had a way of staring down the length of his pert little nose that made Shane feel small. *What the fuck is this guy's problem?*

There was another awkward silence. It seemed to stretch forever, with Kayden looking coolly at Shane, and Shane wringing his hands together and not knowing what the hell to do. It was finally broken by the arrival of Oliver and Surya, the other two members of Moonlight. They, at least, were friendly enough, shaking hands and chatting enthusiastically about the tour.

Shane smiled back gamely and tried to engage himself in the conversation, but his gaze kept returning to Kayden Berlin, who seemed to have a huge chip of ice on his shoulder when it came to the Ventura brothers. Shane only hoped the quiet animosity would die down. Otherwise, it was going to be a long fucking six months.

CHAPTER TWO

"Hey. You ready?" Shane turned to look at Dre, who was standing beside him with his drumsticks in hand, excitedly bouncing on his heels in his usual preconcert tradition.

They were under the stage and set to go on in five minutes. The floor above them practically vibrated with restless energy from the crowd. It stirred Shane's blood and made his heart pound.

He had thought it would fade—that breathless feeling of anticipation he got right before going onstage—but it stayed with him from the very beginning. It was always there, seething beneath the surface. But the nerves that twisted his stomach and made sweat break out on his brow were new. Well, not entirely new. It had just been so long since he'd experienced any type of nervousness about going onstage, he'd almost forgotten how it felt.

The feeling sparked memories of that very first concert, after Luck released their debut album and started their first national tour as the opening act for the After Dark Tour.

Anxiety had made him queasy, and he'd worried for a

while that he'd pull some punk-ass move and pass out onstage. Shane was used to performing for small crowds in dive bars or in auditoriums during school dances, where most of the horny teenagers were too concerned with what might happen afterward to really pay attention to the no-name band providing the soundtrack.

But that night he performed for a crowd of thousands. Fuck, what an adrenaline rush, like the best sex he ever had multiplied by a thousand. There was nothing else like it—being onstage under the lights, feeding off the energy from the screaming fans and the excitement of his bandmates. Knowing that even if most of those people had come to see the headliners, some of them were there to see Luck too.

Shane spent that entire concert in a state of complete euphoria. It was what he'd always wanted, what he'd dreamed of for so many years.

Only afterward, as he came down from the endorphin high in his dressing room, had he been hit by a wave of grief so intense, it doubled him over. Because something was missing that night. *Someone.* The person who'd been instrumental in Luck catching the attention of a record label in the first place. And as Shane sat there, he knew he'd made a mistake; he should have never given in—but it was too late. What he'd done was unforgivable, even if he thought he'd been doing the right thing to ensure his brother's future, to protect him from their abusive asshole of a father. Nothing could be done to take it back. Not ever.

He cried then, alone in that room, in what should have been one of his happiest moments, struck hard by the weight of what he'd lost. No, not lost. Destroyed.

He reached beneath the neckline of his shirt, undid the silver chain around his throat, and tugged it off so he could look at the small shamrock charm that hung suspended from its links. As far as jewelry went, it wasn't very valuable, and when he'd received it as a gift, he played it cool and shrugged it off like it wasn't a big deal. But he'd worn it every day since. Looking at it, he felt a pain in his chest, a slow, steady throb that grew and grew until he curled his fingers around the charm and moaned in sorrow.

Jesse. So sorry....

"Shane? Hey, man, are you in there?"

Shane blinked, snapping back to the present. "Huh?"

"You all right, dude?" Dre asked, eyeing him oddly. "You gonna be okay to go on? Need a pick-me-up?"

Shane shook his head and cleared his throat. "No. No, I'm cool." He nodded to Will, who was already in position on one of the other lifts.

Suddenly, Nick bounded into the area with Em close on his heels. He flung an arm around Shane's shoulders and laughed, jostling him.

"Are you ready for this shit? Our first fuckin' concert with Moonlight. Let's rock this bitch!"

Nick was dressed in a sleeveless, close-fitting denim jacket, which displayed the multiple tattoos decorating his arms to their full advantage. His chest was bare beneath the jacket, the taut skin of his abdomen visible above the low rise of his skinny jeans. His dark-brown hair—normally kept slicked back into what would have been a pompadour style, had it not been shaved on the back and sides—fell into his eyes.

Shane wondered what he was on. Nick looked a bit wild—his face flushed and his pupils wide. Knowing him, it could be just about anything. As long as he performed well, Shane never got on him about his habit of getting high before every concert. In fact, right then, Shane kind of wished he'd taken something himself, something to mellow the nerves rampaging in his stomach.

He knew the reason behind all the anxiety, and it only served to piss him off. Fucking Kayden Berlin. He still didn't know what the hell the guy's problem was. They hadn't spoken much beyond their frosty first meeting, but what both annoyed and confused Shane was the fact that Berlin was so friendly to everyone else.

He was playful with Em, flirting constantly, and even congenial with other members of the band, but with Shane and Nick, he was a goddamn iceberg. Whenever he spoke to them, which he did only when forced, it always seemed like he was peering down his pretty little nose at them both. And Shane had called himself an asshole more than once for even noticing what a pretty nose it was. Kayden never looked at him or his brother with anything but blatant disdain. Instead of checking him out, Shane should be asking him what the deal was.

He couldn't even say why he cared. In the music industry, it was common for artists to collaborate even if they didn't necessarily like each other. It was all about the bottom line. So if Kayden Berlin had some kind of beef with the Ventura brothers, it was no skin off Shane's back. The tour was a business arrangement, nothing more.

But he did care what Berlin thought, and fuck if he knew why. He would've liked to say it was just because he respected the guy as a musician, but normally Shane didn't abide assholes, no matter who they were. And there was no denying Kayden Berlin had been a straight-up prick to both him and Nick since they met a couple of days before. So why couldn't Shane stop thinking about the guy? Why did he find himself watching Berlin whenever the other singer wasn't looking?

Well, it was obvious, really. Lust. Shane wanted to touch him. To bury his fingers in that silky, platinum-blond hair and run his hands over the long, lean lines of Berlin's body. Whenever Kayden walked into a room, Shane's cock stood at attention as if begging to be introduced. He'd already imagined Kayden's mouth on him, taking him in deep and sucking hard, and just the idea of it was enough to make him shudder.

"Places, everyone," one of the backstage crewmembers said. "You're on in ten."

Nick released Shane to go over to the lift that would raise him to the stage. Shane closed his eyes and took a few deep breaths, trying to shake off the nerves. The lift kicked on under his feet, and his stomach drop a bit.

"Make me proud, boys!" Em yelled.

Shane didn't respond; he just kept his eyes shut until the lift stopped. The light show had already begun, but the stage was still mostly dark. He stepped up to the mic, and the energy from the crowd crashed into him, a living and tangible thing. It flowed over him and washed away the anxiety until all that was left was the exhilaration of being onstage. He was in his element in front of an audience, and he thrived on their enthusiasm.

As his bandmates started up the intro to their first song, it was easy to forget about Kayden Berlin, or at least push thoughts of him aside, and get lost in the music. Shane didn't need his guitar for the first number, so he gripped the mic stand and waited for the moment when the spotlights would flare on above him, coinciding with the song's opening line. He heard his cue and started to sing. At that moment, the lights came on, and the crowd went berserk. Screams nearly drowned out the lyrics.

Shane couldn't help but grin, as he glanced over at

Nick, who stood a few feet away. Nick gave a cocky little smile in return, and his right hand was almost a blur as he plucked at the strings of the bass guitar he held. Shane turned back to face the audience and bobbed his head along with the bass line as he sang. All too soon the song was over, and he greeted the crowd in the usual way, thanking them for coming and complimenting their city. He knew the fans weren't there to listen to him talk, so he kept it short, and the band launched into another song immediately afterward.

By the time that song was over, he was sweating. He shrugged off his leather jacket and tossed it aside, leaving the thin white tank top he wore underneath. The next song was one of Luck's heaviest, full of suggestive lyrics about desire, sex, and dominance. Usually he and Will gave the audience a bit of a show while they performed it, though they never really rehearsed what they would do. It varied from one show to the next, which was something the fans loved.

The song, "Touch," built in layers, starting off with an electronic beat, then the drums, the bass, the keyboard, and finally the vocals. The moment the first few words left his lips, the audience went crazy. They knew what was coming, and he wasn't about to disappoint them.

Shane removed the cordless mic from the stand to give himself freedom to move around the stage. He strutted over to Will, whose fingers played gracefully across the keyboard even as he swayed to the beat. Shane circled him, paused to touch, and slipped one hand under the hem of Will's shirt to stroke across his abdomen. Will reached up and grabbed Shane's nape to draw his head down. At the last possible moment, when their lips were just a fraction of an inch from touching, Shane pulled away.

He slowly withdrew his hand from beneath Will's shirt, as if reluctant to give up the contact, and the keyboardist went along with it, leaning into his touch and giving him a hot look from under his fall of dark hair. Seeing that magnified on the jumbo screens on either side of the stage, numerous members of the audience screamed. Shane wanted to laugh. Straight as Will was, he put on a good act.

Shane returned to the center of the stage, all confidence and swagger. Out of the corner of his eye, he saw Nick's hand moving over the neck of his bass guitar as if he were miming giving a hand job. That made Shane want to laugh too. He sang instead, growling out the chorus, guttural and low.

"I wanna do everything to you... hold you down and push into you...." The crowd roared. Shane reached up and grabbed a fistful of his own hair, knowing the action pulled up his shirt, revealing a stripe of sweat-slick skin right above the waistline of his jeans. "Make you scream and beg for it... my touch...."

For a second, he wondered what his father would think of the little performance they put on and the way so many people in the audience ate up the blatant flirting between him and Will. Endless rumors and speculation abounded regarding their supposed relationship. The gossip amused Shane, as did the idea of what his father might think of it all. That is, if that asshole had ever actually seen any of their performances, which Shane doubted.

Shrugging away thoughts of the man, Shane finished the song and moved on to the next. It was the one slow ballad on Luck's set list. The sole romantic ballad in their entire body of work, in fact. He'd written "Absolution" shortly after Luck signed with Blue Horizon. It was about lost love and remorse, and he'd poured his entire soul into the lyrics. None of his bandmates knew who the song was about. None of them even suspected. Only Shane knew. He wrote that song for one person—Jesse.

Shane closed his eyes as he sang; he let the words flow through him. He was surprised to hear his voice tremble on some of the more emotional lines, something that hadn't happened since the very first time he performed the song live.

Maybe it was because Kayden Berlin was out there, possibly watching, probably judging. Berlin—master of the sweeping, emotional ballad. It was one of the things he and Moonlight were best known for. Luck's fan base had been built mainly on their faster-paced, guitar-heavy songs. But "Absolution" *was* a highly personal song for Shane, and for the first time in what felt like years, he wanted it to be perfect.

After that song, the rest of the concert seemed to pass in a blur. They performed a total of thirteen songs in the main set and a two-song encore for the finish. Thunderous applause followed the band as they left the stage. Shane was tired and drenched in sweat, but with the energy buzzing through him, he felt like he could still run a marathon. Nick was already talking about heading to the after-party, but Shane wanted to stay behind. He'd never seen Moonlight play live, and he wanted to see Kayden Berlin in action. He cleaned up in his dressing room and changed into jeans, a fresh T-shirt, and his favorite pair of D&G combat boots.

He'd just finished lacing the boots when his door banged open. He looked up to see Nick leaning against the frame.

"You ready to take off?"

Shane stood and straightened his shirt. "I'm staying."

"What? Why?"

"I want to watch Moonlight."

Nick smirked. "Who's the fangirl now?"

"Shut the hell up," Shane said. He grabbed a bottle of water from the dressing table and unscrewed the cap. "You were the one talking about how brilliant Kayden Berlin is the other day. I'm surprised you're not staying."

"Yeah, that was before the guy started being a total dick." Nick made a derisive sound. "And, speaking of dicks, mine needs servicing."

"That's real classy, Nicky."

Nick grinned. "That's me, all class, all the time. Anyway, if you're not coming, I'm gonna bounce."

"All right. I'll see you back at the hotel."

"Later."

Shane drained his bottle of water and headed toward the greenroom. He wasn't sure if he was hoping Kayden would be there or dreading it, but the question was answered as soon as he opened the door to find the other two members of Moonlight relaxing on one of the couches and the singer conspicuously absent.

Disappointment flared, sudden and intense, and morphed into a feeling of irritation just as quickly. What the hell did it matter if Kayden was there or not? He probably would've just ignored Shane anyway or given him that cool, appraising look that made Shane feel as if Kayden saw right through him and wasn't the least bit impressed with what he found.

"Hey, mate," Surya said as Shane stepped into the room. He held a drink in one hand and a cigarette in the other. "Caught the last bit of your set. Quality, man, pure quality."

"Thanks."

"Care for a fag?"

Startled, Shane blinked for a moment before he remembered "fag" was British slang for a cigarette. "Fuck, yes." He slumped onto the narrow couch next to Surya's and reached for one of the small white cylinders in the box Surya extended toward him. Surya flicked his lighter, and Shane placed the cigarette between his lips and leaned forward to light the tip. He settled back against the couch, sucking in a deep drag. "So where's the boss man?"

"Kayden goes off and does his own thing before every show," Oliver answered. He was seated beside Surya, the latest edition of *Q Magazine* in his hands. "He always just meets us onstage."

"Oh yeah? What's that about?"

"That's just his way, man." Surya shrugged. "We all have our rituals, eh?"

"Look, while I have you two alone, I wanted to ask...." Shane hesitated. "Do you know if Kayden has some sort of problem with me and my brother? He hasn't exactly been friendly, you know what I mean?"

"I noticed." Surya took one last puff of his cigarette and stubbed out the cherry in the ashtray on the coffee table in front of the couch. "But it's a mystery, man. Kayden's a good guy. No joke, he's one of the nicest people I know."

"Yeah," Oliver chimed in. "And this whole tour was his idea. He asked our manager to get in contact with yours."

"Really?" That was news to Shane.

Surya nodded. "Yup."

"But why would he do that if he has some kind of issue with me and Nick?"

"Well, that's the question, innit?" Surya shrugged again. "And I'm afraid I don't have an answer for you, mate. What you reckon, Ollie?"

"No idea." Oliver lowered his magazine to meet Shane's

gaze. "If you really want to know, you should probably just ask him directly."

Shane opened his mouth to answer but was interrupted by a chime from the PA system. The lights in the greenroom flashed three times, and he watched as Surya and Oliver got to their feet.

"Looks like we're up." Surya grinned at him. "Catch you at the after-party."

Shane nodded at them both as they left the room. He stayed behind long enough to finish his cigarette, feeling more confused than ever. The discovery that Kayden Berlin was behind the Lucky Moon Tour had him reeling. Shane had assumed it was something conceived and arranged entirely by their respective labels.

The idea that Kayden initiated the whole thing was a total mind fuck. If he hated—or in the very least *disliked*—both Shane and Nick, then why in the hell would he want them around for a six-month tour? Was it just about the money? But that didn't make sense. It wasn't as if Moonlight's record sales were suffering. And there were other high-profile bands they could have chosen to tour with.

"Fuck, I need to quit thinking about this shit."

Shane ran his fingers through his hair in frustration, mussing the dark strands. He'd slicked it back before the concert, but thanks to his inability to keep his hands off it when he was annoyed, it was back in the unstyled disarray that somehow wound up working for him anyway. He sighed and stood. He'd stayed behind to watch Moonlight, so he might as well go up to the stage. No sense sitting in the greenroom angsting about shit he had no control over.

By the time he made it to the side of the stage, Moonlight had already started their first song. Kayden stood in front of the mic with his trademark glittery blue guitar in hand. He was wearing tight black pants that rode danger-ously low on his hips and a shimmery silver shirt that bared quite a bit of his smooth, toned abdomen. His hair was messy, as if he'd just woken from a nap... or come onstage directly after being thoroughly fucked.

Shane gaped. It took him a few seconds to pick his jaw up off the floor and stop staring. There was no helping the instant hard-on, however. It pressed painfully against the fly of his jeans, and he had to resist the urge to reach down and adjust himself. *What the fuck?* It was like he was thirteen again, popping a boner at the most inconvenient place and time. But, damn. He'd thought the sleek, put-together version of Kayden Berlin was hot. This Kayden was unreal.

Twenty different fantasies flashed through Shane's mind, and he nearly groaned aloud at the last one—of him striding on the stage and taking Kayden right there, under the lights, in front of thousands of fans while the rest of the band played on. He was caught up in the idea of it, rock-hard and throbbing at the mental image, when Kayden began to sing.

Shane's reaction was instantaneous. Kayden's voice washed over him, cooling him down more effectively than a bucket of ice water over his head. The quality of that rich, throaty tenor sent a shiver down his spine.

For a moment, it made him think of Jesse, though Jesse's voice had been higher, less refined. Shane imagined they—Jesse and Kayden—would've sounded great if they'd ever gotten a chance to sing together. The thought was accompa-nied by a dull ache in his gut. He shouldn't be thinking of Jesse, not when it was his fault Jesse wasn't around and would never have a chance to sing a duet with Kayden—or anyone else for that matter. Because Shane and the others had fucked him over. Shane more than anyone. It was

Shane who Jesse had looked at with such pain and betrayal in his eyes. Shane and no one else.

Shane watched the remainder of the concert in a daze. He didn't move from his spot for Moonlight's entire set, which was a couple of songs longer than Luck's had been. His eyes stayed glued to Kayden. The way he played, the way he moved with such elegant, sensual grace, it was as if he'd cast some kind of spell, and Shane was helpless to look away.

For the majority of the concert, Kayden never even glanced his way. Shane thought Kayden either didn't know or didn't care that he stood offstage watching. But then during "Epitaph," Moonlight's longest, piano-intensive ballad, Kayden took a seat at the concert grand that faced his direction.

He sat with his head bowed at first, focused on the keys. It was only when he started to sing that he looked up directly at Shane. Their gazes locked, and Shane felt his breath catch at the power of those sea-green eyes, despite the distance that separated them. In that moment, he realized Kayden had known he was there all along. And as Kayden stared at him unwaveringly, it was like he was singing to Shane. For Shane.

Watch me, his eyes said. *Look at me.*

Shane was looking. Couldn't stop, in fact. Even when Kayden finally broke their connection and turned his attention back to the keys for the intricate piano solo that led to the finish. Shane kept right on looking until the concert was over and the last song had been sung. The members of Moonlight exited the stage past him, Surya grinning and Oliver acknowledging him with a nod. But Kayden brushed by him without so much as a glance.

Shane stood stock-still, fighting back anger and disappointment. What had he expected, really? That the one intense moment they'd shared would have somehow changed Kayden's shitty attitude toward him? Not likely. But Shane knew that whatever animosity Kayden held for him, Kayden had also felt the spark between them burning bright and hot from the instant their eyes met across the hotel conference room two days before. Kayden felt it; Shane had no doubt. Whether or not he would actually admit to it was an entirely different matter.

SHANE KNOCKED BACK the last quarter-inch of tequila in his glass and licked his lips. The liquor was silky smooth as it slid down his throat. He didn't bother with salt or limes. With good tequila, it wasn't necessary, and Shane never wasted his time on inferior liquor. If he was going to get drunk, might as well do it on the quality shit.

He wandered away from the bar toward the balcony, dropping his glass on the tray of a passing waiter. Maybe that last shot had been a bad idea. He'd been skirting the line between pleasantly buzzed and flat-out drunk for most of the night, but he suspected that final mouthful of tequila had pushed him over the edge. The room suddenly seemed hot, stifling. He needed to get out.

Shane stumbled through a pair of french doors onto the balcony, closing his eyes in relief as a cool gust of wind moved over his heated skin. He hadn't seen Nicky in hours, and he had no idea where his other bandmates were. They all seemed to be enjoying the posh after-party on their label's dime, but Shane was bored to tears. He had no interest in any of the people who'd tried to pick him up, male or female. There were always those women who wanted to "convert" him, and no matter how many times he refused, they still persisted.

He was so tired of it all—the ever-present paparazzi and the groupies who hung around hoping to get fucked. But at least they were honest about what they wanted, unlike the people who tried to schmooze their way into his social circle only to stab him in the back at the earliest opportunity. He'd had that happen more than once at the very beginning, which was why he'd decided to out himself instead of waiting for someone to do it for him. He figured if nothing else, maybe the fans would respect him for his honesty.

Shane drew in a few deep breaths, hoping the fresh air would help to clear his head, then turned to go back into the bar. He'd go up to his room and sleep off the alcohol and hopefully his bad mood too.

He'd just made it back to the doors when he felt, more than heard, the dark and seductive chords as if they'd been carried to him by the breeze. The song was melancholy but strangely beautiful. It made the hair on the back of Shane's neck stand on end.

Curious, Shane took a step backward. The song wasn't one he recognized, but he wanted to hear more. He glanced in the direction the music was coming from and saw pale-yellow light spilling out onto the stone tiles from another set of french doors several yards from where he stood. Before he could truly register what he was doing, he'd moved across the balcony to stand beside them.

He found himself looking into some type of lounge. Most of the room was dark, but a few of the lights had been turned on, spotlighting the piano near the bar. Kayden sat before it, his head bowed as he played. He looked intensely focused on the keys despite moving his elegant hands with practiced ease.

As Shane watched Kayden, that strange disconnect between his brain and his limbs happened again. He started moving without conscious thought and was only a few feet away from the piano when Kayden suddenly lifted his head.

Kayden's eyes were closed, and he looked... blissful, his face completely unguarded, his lips curved upward in a serene little smile. The sight of that joyful expression stopped Shane in his tracks and made his heartbeat stall, then kick into overdrive. But as he stood there, frozen in place, staring at Kayden in astonishment, Kayden's eyes slid open and their gazes met.

Surprise flashed across Kayden's face, and then the expression was gone. He returned his gaze to the keys and a few seconds later brought the song to a dramatic conclusion. As the final notes faded, he leaned back, dropping his hands into his lap.

"What was that?" Shane asked when he finally remembered his voice. "It was beautiful."

Kayden brought the cover down over the keys and stroked a hand over its glossy surface. "Rachmaninoff. I've always loved him." He glanced up at Shane, his expression cool. "What are you doing here?"

"I was out on the balcony, and I heard the music. I got curious."

"Ah." Kayden stood and tucked the piano bench into place. "I'm surprised you're still down here. I would've thought you'd be upstairs in your room by now with a trio of followers, like your brother."

Shane shrugged. "I'd rather be here talking to you."

Kayden gave a dry laugh. "That's a good line."

"It's not a line."

"Of course not." Kayden looked away from Shane, toward the doors that led to the balcony. "I need some air."

He walked away without waiting for Shane to respond.

Shane felt a flicker of annoyance at being so summarily dismissed. He didn't stop to think; he just followed Kayden out into the moonlit night. The other singer had already crossed to the railing and was leaning against it, his gaze focused on the skyline.

Shane moved to stand beside him and crossed his arms over his chest. But he wasn't interested in the view, as gorgeous as it was. The only thing he saw was Kayden. In the moonlight, Kayden's white-blond hair took on an ethereal glow. Shane's fingers itched to reach out and touch it, see if it was as soft as he imagined.

Kayden glanced sideways at him, his eyes the color of emeralds in the darkness. "Was there something else you wanted?"

Well, that's a loaded question. Shane had about a dozen answers on the tip of his tongue, but he settled on saying what had been on his mind since he watched Kayden perform that night. "You were awesome earlier. I think you put on the best live show I've ever seen. Your voice... it's incredible."

Kayden looked away, back out toward the city. He stayed quiet for a moment in a silence that seemed loud with all of the things Shane wished he could say.

"Thank you," Kayden said finally.

"Tonight felt different from a lot of the concerts I've done recently. You know how it is, when you're constantly on the road doing show after show. It starts to feel like a job. Sometimes it's hard for me to give a shit what we sound like, but tonight—"

"It never feels like a job for me," Kayden interrupted coldly. "I love it. Being able to tour, to play for my fans, just the fact that I can say I *have* fans—that's a privilege. People put down their hard-earned money to watch us perform. I *never* take it lightly."

"Look, I know, I—I didn't mean for it to sound like I don't appreciate the fans. I do. I know how many bands don't make it. I know we're lucky—"

Kayden muttered under his breath, something that sounded like "You have no idea."

"What was that?"

Kayden shook his head without looking at him. "Nothing."

"I'm sorry, okay? That came out wrong. I just... I was trying to say that I felt inspired earlier. Like revitalized, you know? It got me to thinking, maybe after the tour is over, we can collaborate on something. With your voice—"

"No. I'm not interested." Kayden's voice was harsh, his cultured accent thicker than normal.

"But Oliver and Surya told me you were the one who wanted to tour with Luck, that you asked your manager to contact Em."

Kayden glanced at him then and gave a nonchalant shrug. "So?"

"So?" Shane repeated, incredulous. "If you don't have any interest in working with Luck, why would you want to tour with us?"

"You're reading too much into the situation. It's simple. I wanted to do a joint tour with another band, I knew we were both releasing albums this spring, and I thought our styles would mesh well."

"And that's it?"

"That's it."

Shane shook his head. "I find that hard to believe. There were other bands you could have picked."

Kayden shrugged. "Believe what you want."

Shane glanced skyward for patience and heaved an exasperated sigh. "I don't get you."

"You don't have to *get* me. You don't even have to speak to me."

"Yeah." Shane looked down into those deep-green eyes, searching for a crack in Kayden's icy exterior. He wished he could tell what Kayden was thinking, but the other singer regarded him steadily, his expression a blank wall that gave nothing away. "You've made that perfectly clear, haven't you?"

"Yes," Kayden said. "So why can't you seem to take the hint?"

Stunned, Shane could only stare at him. Kayden flicked a brief, dismissive glance over him and turned on his heel. Before Shane could think of something to say, he was gone. And so was Shane's buzz.

Shane faced the stone railing and gripped it to still the sudden trembling in his hands as he gazed out over the city without really seeing anything. An indefinable emotion settled heavily in his stomach, and he swallowed against the accompanying queasiness. He had no idea why the opinion of a complete stranger had affected him so strongly. He buried his fingers in his hair and tugged at the strands in aggravation. Who was Kayden Berlin anyway? *Fuck him.*

Too bad that even as pissed off as he was, it was still the only thing Shane wanted to do. Fuck Kayden Berlin.

CHAPTER THREE

Then....
Chicago

"I'm fucking tired of this math shit, Jesse. It's hot, and I wanna go to the skate park."

Jesse gave Shane one of his unwavering looks, the ones he knew were the best way to drive Shane completely out of his mind.

As always, Shane caved beneath the weight of his stare. He grunted and looked down at his math book again.

"Why can't we go back to the science stuff? That makes sense at least. It isn't just some big-ass pile of random numbers." He frowned, his forehead creasing.

Jesse fought back a sigh. He knew how frustrated Shane got with equations—and, really, math wasn't Jesse's favorite subject either—but they were *so close*. If Shane could only focus, Jesse didn't doubt he could breeze through this, no sweat. The problem was Shane's lack of confidence—and how quick he was to get angry and give up when he didn't understand something.

"Shane, you can get this. I promise. You've only got, what, like four weeks till graduation? Then you're done. *Done.* And you don't have to deal with math or me ever again. Come on. Look at the problem. I'll go through it one more time."

Shane kicked the empty chair next to him. "I don't like to be hot."

"And I don't like babies. I'm hot too. But you're finally passing this class thanks to those labs Mr. Lopez let you do over. Don't spoil it now. Let's just get this done so we can get out of here. Look, this one is just a matter of percentages."

Shane frowned even harder, his full mouth turned downward. "What? You know I don't get all these math words."

Jesse thought for a moment. "Okay, look. Let's take... The Sex Pistols, right? So if they had a concert at, uh, say Wembley Stadium in London and they sold eighty-five percent of the tickets—"

"Don't patronize me by using things I'll 'understand.'" Shane made little quotes in the air with his fingers. "Just 'cause I look like a punk doesn't mean I'm into that shit."

Annoyed, Jesse said, "Well, I am, and it's the best example I could come up with."

Shane looked floored, his blue eyes wide. "You're into punk? Wow, just when you think you know a guy."

"Yeah, and grunge and alternative and almost everything else. I'm not picky. I love music. I've played the piano most of my life, and I play guitar too."

"Really? What made you get into piano?"

Jesse made a face. "My mom at first. She wanted me to be the next Mozart—even made my middle name Amadeus." Shane snickered, and Jesse smiled along with him. "I know, right? I hardly ever tell anyone that. Anyway, it wasn't love at first sight. Learning chords and scales was boring, and I hated it, but as soon as the real music started...." Jesse broke off with a happy sigh.

"Then it was love?"

Jesse nodded. "Then it was love."

"So piano and guitar, huh? Can you sing?"

"Sure." Jesse shrugged.

"And you're really into alt-rock and grunge and shit?" Shane asked, his expression making it clear he was having a hard time buying it. "Huh. You don't look like much of a rocker."

Jesse chuckled.

"What?"

"I was going to say you don't look like much of an asshole, but sometimes you really do."

Shane laughed. "Sorry, dude. I guess I earned that one. Still learning that 'not judging by what you see' thing."

"It's cool. We'll keep working on it. Maybe someday you'll realize I'm not the big pencil pusher you think I am."

"No kidding. Think I'm on my way."

Jesse smiled. "So you want to finish this math?"

Shane shut his math book and gave Jesse that gorgeous grin that always made his pulse kick up a few notches. "No, I wanna talk about music. You really play guitar?"

Jesse shook his head, but his smile widened as he closed his own book. He knew he shouldn't let himself be distracted, but no way could he resist that grin, and Shane had found the one subject Jesse loved above all others. A little break wouldn't hurt anything, he told himself, so long as he helped Shane finish his assignment later.

"Yeah. I have a six-string acoustic and an electric. My

mom just about has a donkey every time I plug in my electric, but God, I love playing that thing."

Shane was silent for a few seconds. Then he chuckled softly. "Yeah, my mom would've probably had a donkey herself."

Abruptly, a thought popped into Jesse's head. A laugh escaped him before he could squelch it, startling in the quiet murmur of the library.

Shane looked at him curiously. "What this time?"

"Well, I was just going to say it's hard to picture you with a mother, but then I realized I was wrong. You are so a momma's boy."

"Fuck off. I am not."

"Mmm-hmm. Does the whiny act work with her when you don't want to do something?"

Shane's expression darkened. After a long moment, he said, "No. I don't have a mother anymore. She's gone."

"Oh." Guilt twisted in Jesse's stomach. He wished more than anything he could take the words about Shane's mother back. "Is she...?"

"Dead?" Shane shook his head. "Nah. She took off when I was in fourth grade. Haven't seen her since."

Jesse could tell Shane meant his answer to sound like he didn't give a shit about his mom leaving, but the tension in his voice was obvious. Jesse bit his lip to stop himself from asking all the questions in his head.

"I'm sorry," he said instead. "Who do you live with?"

"My dad. He's an asshole. He works most of the time, though, thank God."

"So did you basically raise Nick?" Jesse asked. Shane's brother was a freshman, a couple of years behind Jesse. And notorious for constantly getting into trouble.

"You know Nicky?" Shane asked, surprised.

Jesse gave him a disbelieving look. "The whole school knows him. He mooned the homecoming procession at the pep rally last semester."

Shane laughed. "Oh, I forgot about that. Guess you do know him, and yeah, I did. The brat was a handful. Still is."

"That's really cool that you take care of your brother like that. See? There's a good guy hidden under that badass exterior." Jesse chuckled softly.

"Ha. And to think I was just about to ask you to come jam with us...." Shane shook his head sadly. "See, we're getting a band together, and we need a lead singer and a second guitar. It's really too bad. Could've been you."

"You want me to play with you?" Jesse couldn't help his excited grin. How awesome would it be to practice with a *real* band for once instead of just in his room by himself? He'd never had the opportunity before. None of his friends had any real interest in rock music.

Shane lifted one shoulder in a casual shrug. "I did, but we can't have any shit-talking, you know? Bandmates have gotta be loyal to each other. Like family." Shane sighed dramatically and went to open his math book again.

Jesse reached out a hand to stop him. "Shane? I'm sorr—"

Shane looked up at him, his serious expression vanishing as he burst into chuckles. "You should see the look on your face, kid." He made a mocking pathetic pout. "Of course you can come practice with us. I wanna see what you can do. Is there any way you can lose the glasses, though? My brother's going to give you such shit for those."

"I can't see a thing without them."

"Shit. Well, stand behind me till we know everything's kosher. Nick's a bit—"

"Yeah, I get it," Jesse interrupted with a slight wince. "Don't worry."

"C'mon. I'll finish the math later." Shane glanced at the clock on the wall above the doors. "They should just be leaving the skate park and heading home now."

Stunned, Jesse watched as Shane shoved his supplies into his backpack and stood. "You want me to meet them today?"

Shane shrugged. "Why not? I'm here, you're here, they're there. It all works out. Let's go."

Jesse trembled a little, sudden nerves making his skin clammy. Shane must've noticed because he reached out and gave him a reassuring pat on the back.

"It'll be cool," Shane said. "Oh, and no matter what Nicky says to you, I didn't tie him to his bed last summer and try to wax his nuts."

Jesse laughed, just as he knew Shane had intended. His stomach was going crazy, but he gamely packed his bag and followed as Shane led the way out of the library to the freedom of the outdoors.

"I think I'm going to regret this."

SHANE WAS EMBARRASSED to bring Jesse into his neighborhood. It wasn't the nicest, for sure. Not exactly the ghetto, but you wouldn't want to be caught walking around alone at night. The families were mainly Mexican, though there were a few Puerto Rican families like his thrown in. A lot of the houses had weedy, overgrown lawns and paint jobs that needed to be redone years ago. Most of the yards were surrounded by chain-link fence, and at least half of those had some big dog that would scare the shit out of you if you weren't paying attention when you walked by.

Jesse didn't seem to notice the area, though. He seemed to be too wrapped up in his own nerves to worry about much other than himself. That was fine with Shane. He had enough to think about already. When Jesse asked about his mother earlier, he'd expected to shut down, as he always did when he thought about her. Instead, he found himself tempted to tell Jesse everything, which was just weird as hell. Shane never talked about her. Ever. He hated her every day for leaving them with their asshole of a father. So why was there something about Jesse that made him want to spill the whole sad story?

"Hey, we're here." He nudged Jesse toward his house.

Between him and his dad, they kept the place in much better shape than most of the other houses on the block. He tried to keep the yard neat, and they usually put a new coat of white on the front trim at least every other summer. It was still small, though, and for all he knew, Jesse was from some awesome neighborhood with no gang problems or corner drug dealers.

"Cute place," Jesse told him with a tremulous smile.

"Thanks." Shane shook his head at the word *cute*. "You'll be fine, by the way."

"Yeah, you think?"

"I do. Dre's actually pretty cool, and Nicky, Well, just ignore him. I usually do."

"Great."

"C'mon." Shane led Jesse in through the front door with a hand on his lower back. Jesse's shirt was warm under his fingertips, and Shane's stomach did an odd little flip. *What the fuck?* He pushed the flip down as far as he could. *I'm just hungry, that's all.* His thoughts were interrupted by an angry face poking around the kitchen doorjamb. *Fuck. He's supposed to be at work already.*

"Hey, uh, Pop. This is Jesse. He's been tutoring me at school."

"What for? The Venturas are fuckups. Always have been, always will be. Will you go tell your brother to turn his goddamn speakers down? I'm trying to have a few fucking moments of peace before I go to work."

"Yeah, Pop. No problem."

"I've got a double shift tonight. I won't be back until late morning. Keep that little shit out of trouble. Can I trust you to do that?"

Shane only nodded, embarrassed beyond belief that anyone was meeting his father. He tried to keep everyone away from the mean-tempered old bastard. Especially Jesse. He hadn't wanted Jesse to see any of this. *Why the fuck not? What is my problem all of a sudden?* Shane shook it off and tried to act like nothing was feeling different. Weird. Floaty. *Fuck.*

"Jay, let's go downstairs, and I'll introduce you to the guys."

"Jay?"

"Fine. Jesse. Let's go."

They clomped down the narrow, rickety stairs to the basement. Shane reached out and gripped the wall. He was always half afraid he was going to wipe out someday and kill himself on the dumb things.

His boys sat at the bottom of the stairs, waiting for him, listening to Pearl Jam, and smoking a bowl.

"Shit, Nicky. Put that away. Dad's still home."

His cocky son of a bitch brother's face dropped, and he started putting out the smoking pipe. "I thought I heard him leave."

Shane shook his head. His brother never learned. It wouldn't have been the first time either of them got their asses beat by their father. Shane was determined that soon it would be the last, though. Make enough money, get Nicky the hell out of the house. He wanted out himself, but he wasn't going to leave without his brother.

"I couldn't smell it upstairs. He said to turn the speakers down too. We're gonna have to wait till he leaves to start practicing." Shane gestured to Jesse. "Nicky, Dre, this is Jesse. I think he's our missing member."

Nick gave Jesse a long look-over. "What's up with you, Shaney? First you tell me you're a queer, and now this? The pocket-protector squad?"

Shane saw Jesse's eyes widen. Great. That was not how he'd planned on breaking the news. "You know what, Nicky? You can fuck off. I told you I'd find us someone. I think Jesse's it."

Nick stood, grabbed an acoustic from the corner, and handed it to Jesse. "Fine. Let nerd-wad here show us what he can do."

Jesse blushed and took the guitar. He sat on the old painted stool that was in the corner and started strumming and checking the tuning. Then he played the guitar intro to an old Beatles song, one of Shane's favorites, before he started to sing. The moment his voice filled the room, the back of Shane's neck burst into goose bumps. His voice was a high tenor, gorgeous, throaty, and mellow. It seemed to travel into all the little corners of the basement until it hit Shane right in the gut. He listened raptly, just like Dre and Nick, who sat silently until the song was over.

It took a few moments before he realized Jesse was waiting for a reply. Shane made a coughing noise to clear the odd tightness in his throat. *Don't you dare get fucking teary over a dumb song.* He stood for a moment, trying to get his shit together before he spoke to Jesse, who all of a sudden was someone completely different. It was actually Nick who spoke first.

"Uh, yeah, dude. You're in."

That worked. It was what Shane was trying to say anyway.

Now....
Berlin

"Welcome to Berlin, boys."

Em ushered them from the small plane that had flown them from Paris to Amsterdam, then on to Berlin before they headed north into Scandinavia. Em winked at Kayden, who winked back and gave Luck's flirtatious little manager a huge smile.

The night still had a bit of a bite. Spring hadn't quite translated to warmth yet in the northern latitudes. Shane didn't mind. The fresh air actually cleared his head from the staleness in the little plane.

His head had been alarmingly clear for the past three and a half weeks. He hadn't been able to lose himself in a haze of anything without seeing Kayden's piercing eyes in the back of his mind, so he gave up. Somewhere outside of Glasgow, Shane Ventura had embraced sobriety.

Reluctantly.

His nights lately were spent on his own, in his room, actually sleeping. The other night he even got out a book to read, for fuck's sake. Shane didn't know what his world was coming to. He wished he didn't feel better for it. But he did.

"Hopefully it'll be a good show. Berlin should be good luck for me. My mother was born here." Kayden's voice startled Shane a bit, and he nearly tripped on the last step before hitting the hard tarmac.

"Like you could put on a bad show." Em batted at Kayden's arm.

True. Moonlight had been amazing every single night. Shane would know. He watched from the side of the stage for each show, never tiring of listening to Kayden's intoxicating voice.

"Kayden, this is your car, and Shane—what the hell?" That last bit was whispered. Em whipped out his smartphone and hit a few buttons before putting the phone to his ear. His foot tapped impatiently as he waited for an answer. "Where is Mr. Ventura's car?" he demanded seconds later. "That's not acceptable. No. *No*. We don't want to wait for another."

Shane held out his hand. "Em, it's fine. I'll ride with Kayden." He inclined his head at the car where Kayden was crawling in, showing a few inches of creamy pale lower back as his shirt rode up.

Shane gulped. *Shit, he's hot. Cold as ice, but hot all the same.* Too bad he mostly hated the haughty Kayden Berlin, because he would definitely love to get in the guy's pants. Well, at least he wanted the guy that Kayden was to everyone else. He still didn't get what he and Nicky had done to make him act like such an asshole to them. Kayden's bandmates either didn't know, or they weren't telling. Whatever. He stalked over to the limo and slid in behind Kayden.

"What are you doing in here?" The voice was the same as always. Bored, aloof, hot as hell.

"My car didn't show. You'll have to lower yourself to accepting my presence for just a few minutes."

Kayden shrugged and stretched slowly. His glittery T-shirt rode up with the movement, revealing the long, flat plane of his stomach.

"Suit yourself," he said with a yawn. They heard the trunk slam shut, and moments later the car pulled away from the loading area and started in the direction of their hotel.

"Drink?" Kayden asked once the limo was en route. "My ex taught me how to make a perfect whiskey sour, and I see we have the right ingredients."

"Uh, sure. Ex?" There had never been any concrete reports of Kayden Berlin dating anyone, although rumors about his sexuality had been circulating for years.

"Yeah. He said the trick was in the shaking."

He. Well, then, that mystery is solved.

"I am gay. I could tell you wanted to ask. I just don't make it as public of a... spectacle... as you do." Kayden crinkled up his flawless nose in a show of disdain.

Shane tried to ignore the shot of heat to his groin that came when he thought of the fact that Kayden Berlin slept with men. God, he could just picture him, arched off a bed, his creamy white skin glowing, Shane's hard—*fuck.*

Shane tried to remind himself that he hated the guy, and it didn't matter how hot or how gay Kayden Berlin was, he seemed to hate Shane back. He reached up and fingered the shamrock around his neck, something he did every time he was feeling unsure of himself. For one of the first times, though, the action didn't conjure Jesse's face. All he could see was Kayden: in his bed, in his arms, in his body. *Fuck again. That's even worse.* If there was one thing Shane Ventura didn't do, it was bottom. Ever. He had no idea what his problem was.

Kayden crawled over to the bar area. His designer jeans slipped down as he moved so just the top of his pretty round little butt was on display. Shane wanted to reach out and cup the flesh in his hand, to see if it felt as warm as it looked, to trace the curve with his tongue and taste all the hidden places. He pressed his nails into the palm of his hand, trying to stop the barrage of mental images.

When Kayden returned with two drinks balanced precariously in his hands, he must've noticed the draft on his bare skin. He laughed shyly for a moment, his arrogant mask falling away like he forgot he had to have it, and passed Shane a drink before he settled down with his own. He shifted awkwardly in his seat, using his free hand to tug up one side of his waistband at a time.

"Sorry. That was a bit more than I'd planned on showing there. These jeans always fall down."

His smile was so sweet. Directed at Shane for the first time, it was devastating. Lust and desire blindsided Shane, and something more burned in his gut. *Shit.* How was he supposed to have a lust/hate relationship with someone who smiled like that? It was the sweetest thing he'd ever seen.

Kayden seemed to notice Shane watching him and brought his hand up to cover his smile. The gesture was uncomfortably familiar.

"Hey, you've got a great smile. Don't hide it."

Shane's words seemed to spark a reaction in Kayden. The haughty mask slipped back into place, cool and beautiful. He stretched again, eyeing Shane the whole time as if he knew exactly how much Shane liked to look at him.

"Uh, what just happened there?" Shane was tired of whatever crap was between them.

"What do you mean?" Kayden looked bored, but Shane thought his boredom was a pretense. He'd seen the cracks in

Kayden's armor. He wanted to know why the armor was there in the first place.

"I mean, for ten seconds you weren't being an asshole, and now the asshole's back. What gives?"

"Maybe I find you boring."

"Maybe you're full of shit. There is fucking *lightning* between us. All it took was me walking into that room back at the meeting. No one else existed for either of us."

Kayden rolled his eyes. "Those must have been some great drugs you were on."

"I wasn't on drugs then, and I'm not on them now. I can feel it between us."

Kayden huffed and lounged back into the plush leather seat.

"You know, you're not as unaffected by me as you like to pretend," Shane went on. "Whenever you get upset, you have to concentrate on talking. You're doing it now."

"Well, it's good to know you're stalking me." Kayden's tone was droll, but his voice trembled a bit.

"You drive me crazy."

"You need something better to do, then."

"*Argh.* What is your fucking problem with me?" Shane was practically yelling.

Those weeks in the UK had been excruciating, watching the man in front of him come alive onstage, all sex and glamour and talent, laughing and flirting with his friends, then turning around and treating Shane with such cold disdain. He wanted a reason. He needed a reason.

"My problem?"

"*Yes.* Your problem. Why are you mister nice guy with everyone else but a flaming asshole to me?"

"Not just you."

"Nicky too. *Fuck.* Can you just tell me what either one

of us did to your royal rock 'n' roll highness to make you act like you do?"

"With him, it's simple. I don't like him. With you, it's more."

"What? So you don't like me, *and* you've got some insults to pile on top of that? Wonderful."

"You're a train wreck, okay? A cliché. Every joke that's ever been told about aging badasses and you don't even know how sad you are. Yes, I'm attracted to you. No, I don't want to do anything about it. I hate that my body reacts to yours, because I want nothing to do with the mess that is Shane Ventura. *Nothing.*"

Shane sat back against the seat cushions, reeling. *God, that sucked.* He wished he could take it back, unask the questions, get the hell out of that fucking limousine, and never have to see the man in front of him again. Humiliation crushed the air right out of him.

"And you know the worst part?" Kayden went on before Shane could reply. "You could have been one of the great ones. The potential was there in the beginning, but you've fucked it all away."

After that, he fell silent, and Shane too stopped speaking, not wanting to know any more of how Kayden, and probably people everywhere, saw him. It hurt, deep in his gut, a burning pain that was the knowledge of what he'd become.

All Shane knew was he couldn't wait for their damn tour to be over so he'd never have to look at Kayden's face again.

CHAPTER FOUR

Then...
Chicago

"Ugh. Shane, I don't think this was such a good idea."

Shane looked over at his friend. Jesse didn't look too hot. Luck was waiting backstage, ready to go on. It wasn't the time for important band members to freak out. Jesse _couldn't_ freak out. He was the band's lead singer and owner of one of the most gorgeous voices Shane had ever heard. Without him, Luck might never have gotten a gig, even if it _was_ just for some crappy school dance.

Jesse leaned over at the waist and made a few rather loud retching sounds.

Ah shit. Don't puke, Jess.

The kid was made for music, _born_ to sing, but the stage, on the other hand? It didn't look like the stage was going to be Jesse's friend. Probably not the best moment to find that out. It was Luck's first performance. Ever. (Unless you count a few cans of Mountain Dew on his dad's basement floor as an audience.) Nerves were to be expected. Puking wouldn't be so great, though. Best to avoid the puking.

"Jess, you're gonna be fine. You sing like a frickin' angel and you play the guitar like fire. Just get the hell out there and show those kids who Jesse Seider is."

"Jesse Seider isn't anybody," he groaned. "It would be a hell of a lot cooler if I had a last name like yours."

"Ventura's not so special. Your voice is." Shane rubbed Jesse between the shoulders. It was an uncharacteristically soft gesture for him. He tried not to let people in. Jesse was different. He managed to sneak in right from the start.

"Look at 'em, Shaney." Nick gestured to the crowd of disinterested teenagers on the other side of the curtain. "I can't believe we're playing cover tracks at a high-school dance. This blows my *ass*."

"*Nick*." Dre thwacked him with a drumstick. "They probably heard that in Timbuktu. Do you *have* an inside voice?"

Nick guffawed. "Have I ever?"

Shane took another glance at Jesse. Looked like Nick and Dre's usual arguing antics had distracted him from the nausea. *Good*.

"Ready, Freddie?" Shane asked him with a small nudge of his hips.

"Don't call me Freddie," Jesse joked weakly. Then he did a few warm-up strums on his guitar and nodded.

Shane supposed it didn't much matter anyway. Ready or not, they were on. The somewhat damp red velvet curtain was raised, and the sea of students suddenly seemed a whole helluva lot closer. Shit. And he thought Jesse was nervous.

I can do this.

An old guy in a suit—the principal, probably—cleared

his throat into the mic. "Ahem, students and faculty of Cabrini Heights, will you please join me in a warm round of applause for...." He shuffled a stack of papers.

"Are you fucking kidding me?" Nicky's inside voice wasn't any quieter than the last time. A few students snickered behind their hands. Nicky stepped forward and grabbed the microphone. "We're Luck, and we're going to rock you!"

Nicky's shout was met with scattered applause. They had to keep going as if they'd gotten a stadium full of screams. Dre counted them down with his sticks on the rim of his snare, and they were on. Too late to go back.

Their first few chords were greeted with indifference, but one by one the students warmed up. Luck started with a rocked-out version of "Johnny B. Goode." Everyone knew that song, right? It was their chance. If they didn't have the crowd with the first song, they wouldn't have them at all.

Shane played lead guitar, and Jesse kept up a driving rhythm over Nicky's complicated bass. Shane was terrified at first, but when Jesse's voice came in loud and strong, he started to breathe... and perhaps even have a little bit of fun. Nick showboated around the stage like only he could, thrusting with his hips under his bass and making the girls in the front row squeal.

They had them, goddammit. This room of high-school kids was going to be theirs.

"Johnny B. Goode" ended with enthusiastic applause. They segued quickly into The Cure's "Just Like Heaven," with Jesse on keyboards and Shane singing lead, before slowing it down with a perfect copy of Pearl Jam's cover of "Last Kiss." Nick took over and sang Eddie Vedder's lead vocals in his low, gravelly voice, which was sure to make the girls swoon. Jesse and Shane played the two guitars off each other, harmonizing and trading riffs. There were kids in the audience slow dancing; some were just watching the band. Shane knew some of those girls were staring at him. One of them winked. Shane wanted to roll his eyes, but he smiled right back at the girl flirtatiously. Had to play the crowd.

Shane looked over at Jesse and grinned. Jesse knew how girls were with him. He also knew that Shane couldn't care less. He was never going to be into a girl. Ever. Shane was happy to leave them to his brother. Jesse chuckled and shook his head.

Jess.

Just watching him play made Shane smile. He couldn't ask for a better best friend. They hadn't even known each other for a year yet, but it already felt like Jesse had always been an important part of his life. And now, with Jess, Shane knew Luck was finally heading somewhere special. Somewhere *big*. How could they go in any direction but up with a talent like Jesse's in their mix? It would only be a matter of time before they were discovered. Shane had faith.

"What's next?" Jesse whispered when they finished the Pearl Jam cover.

"'Buddy Holly,'" Shane answered.

Weezer. It was one of his favorites. He'd been looking forward to it. Shane threw the distortion pedal on his amp and waited for a count-in from Dre on the drums.

By the time Jesse was done with the first line, Shane was full out grinning. The nerves were gone. In that musty old gym, on the stage with his brother and his best friends in the world, he was having the time of his life. Who cared if it was just some high school kids bopping their heads to Weezer on the floor of a basketball court instead of a Luck original at Madison Square Garden? Those days would come. He was sure of it. He and Jesse could do anything.

They worked their way through Sugar Ray's surfy "Someday," singing to each other and the crowd. Nicky's favorite came next. All it took was him growling "The world is a vampire" into the mic, and the girls just lost it. Shane was proud. His brother sure as hell knew how to do what needed to be done.

JESSE COULDN'T BELIEVE IT. He was on stage. *Singing.* And it was okay. Fun, even.

He'd been sure he wasn't going to make it to the front of the stage without puking his guts out all over the crowd. Good thing he hadn't eaten earlier when his mom tried to shove lunch down his throat. It would've come up so damn fast.

The first song or two were a little awkward, but by the time they started on Sugar Ray, he was having an honest-to-God good time. All it took sometimes was one of those big, gorgeous smiles from Shane, and he felt like he could do anything. And there it was. That smile. They swayed together with the beachy beat, and Shane looked right at him and mouthed "you were always there for me" right with the lyrics.

Aw shit. Why's he gotta be gay?

Jesse felt a bolt in his stomach. *Music, asshole. Play the music.* But it was true. It would've been so much easier not to have the world's most ridiculous never-gonna-happen crush on his best friend if there wasn't that one little niggling hint of *maybe.*

"Jess... 'Till There Was You.' Let's do it." Jesse's stomach dropped. Everything had gone so well. "Till There

Was You" was a classic. It would be only him and Shane, no electrics, no drums. Terrifying. He went to shake his head, but Shane nodded significantly. "C'mon, Jess. It's perfect."

Jesse nodded, not sure of it at all, and turned to pick his electrical acoustic off its stand. Shane followed suit and nodded for Dre and Nick to take a break. Jesse raised his eyebrows at Shane.

I might be playing the damn song, but you're going to do the talking.

Shane grinned at him and stepped up to his microphone. "This is the first song I ever heard Jesse sing." He smiled engagingly at the audience. "I'm pretty sure you'll see why we hired him." Then he winked and turned to Jesse. "Ready?"

No. "Let's do this."

They started out with the complex, two guitar cha-cha rhythm. Jesse only had a few eight counts before he had to come in. *Deep breath. You got it. Go.*

He sang the first verse on his own before Shane joined in on backup. Jesse's voice rang out across the auditorium, stripped down and in his perfect range. He was singing for Shane. He always sang for Shane—like a loser. Jesse wished it didn't affect him so much when Shane smiled at him the way he did. After eight months, he'd come to accept it.

The concert ended with tons of applause and two encores. It barely felt real. The curtain closed on them slowly (ending with Nick sticking his head out and blowing kisses to a group of giggling girls). After they were hidden from view, Shane whooped softly and ran over to engulf Jesse in a huge hug.

"You did it, dude," he whispered. Jesse heard the pride in Shane's voice.

"We all did."

"Yeah, but your voice was perfect." Shane ruffled his hair in the seconds before they were bombarded by hugs from Dre and Nick.

"We rocked that fucker!" Nick crowed. Loudly, of course. It was good that the thumpa thump of the bass from the DJ covered his voice—and his rather impressive vocabulary. Shane shoved him.

"What, dude? We've gotta go *celebrate.*"

"Not too late. You've got school on Monday. So does Jesse." Shane's voice sounded like the law.

Unimpressed, Nick sneered. "Fuck you. Just 'cause you barely managed to graduate doesn't make you king of the world."

Jesse sighed. If they got Nick out of high school successfully, it would be a miracle.

"Shane's right. I have a project to finish up tomorrow, and I'm sure you have homework you need to do. We can go out for pizza or something, though."

Jesse was treated an eye roll. "I always knew you were a loser. Why'd you gotta make my brother one too?"

Jesse shrugged. He didn't take Nick too seriously.

Shane tossed his arm around Jesse's shoulders. "We can be losers together," he whispered, loud enough to make sure Nick heard him. Nick flipped him off. "Let's go get a large pepperoni and talk about how amazing we are and how we're going to book a ton of shows this winter."

Jesse chuckled to cover up the fact that his back had burst into a cascade of goose bumps. *Shane, you have no idea.* And he never would. Jesse just grinned and said, "Yeah, let's go get pizza."

They walked out into the chill of a late fall night. There were stars glittering above the city, and the cool breeze was a relief after the stuffiness in the gym. Jesse smiled. It was their first show together, but hopefully just the first of many. Jesse felt like he was ready to take over the world, and he wanted to do it with Shane by his side. Shane might never find out how he felt, but that didn't change anything. Their band was going to make it big. They had to. Luck was too good just to fade into nothing. Jesse wouldn't allow it.

But no matter what, big or small, world tours or holidays at home in Chicago, he, Shane, Nick, and Dre were a team. They were going to do it all—together.

Now....
Rome

"YES. RIGHT THERE."

Shane looked up at Kayden's face. The singer's eyes were closed, his pale skin darkened with a delicate flush, his lips slick from the kiss they'd just shared. His bare chest rose and fell in time with his quick breathing.

"You like that?" Shane leaned forward to flick his tongue over a small pink nipple and pressed his fingers deeper into Kayden's body. He curled them upward and found the spot he was searching for, circling the bundle of nerves with a slow, persistant touch.

Kayden hissed, arching his back off the carpet. "Yeah."

Shane licked a path across Kayden's chest to his other nipple and tongued it, moving his fingers in a steady rhythm, stretching and flexing Kayden's tight inner muscles. Shane couldn't wait to be inside, to feel those muscles gripping his cock, pulling him in. He was already painfully hard, straining against the fly of his jeans. He didn't think it was possible for him to get any harder, but when Kayden moaned and pressed down against his hand, fucking himself with Shane's fingers, Shane's erection stiffened even further.

"Oh fuck." Shane ground himself against Kayden's hip, his eyes locked on the other singer's face. Kayden had tossed his head back, exposing the graceful column of his throat. His expression of agonized pleasure went straight to Shane's cock. He couldn't remember the last time he was so turned on and desperate to fuck. Probably not since he discovered what sex was all about as a teenager. But he'd never wanted anyone this much before. "That's it. Take it. Take what you want."

"I want you," Kayden whispered, his voice rough with desire. "I need you in me."

Shane was only too happy to oblige. He couldn't resist an appeal like that, the impatient demand in Kayden's voice. He withdrew his fingers, quickly undid his jeans, and shoved them down far enough for his dick to spring free. Things were a bit awkward, sprawled out on the floor in the back of the limo as they were, but Shane managed to get Kayden's pants stripped off. He threw them up onto the leather seat and settled between Kayden's thighs, placing his hands on Kayden's knees to spread his legs wide.

He'd sucked on his fingers earlier before working them into Kayden, but Shane knew that wasn't really enough to ease his way, at least not without causing pain. Lacking conveniences like lube or even lotion, he did what he had to —spit into his hand and used that to slick his cock. He positioned himself at Kayden's entrance and looked up at his face. Kayden's eyes were still closed. He was trembling and worrying at his lower lip with his teeth.

"Open your eyes," Shane commanded softly. "Look at me." Kayden did as he asked. Their gazes met. "Watch me...." Shane leaned forward to brace a hand on the floor next to Kayden's shoulder; with the other he held his cock steady. For once, Kayden didn't glance away. He kept his eyes on Shane's, tilting his hips up as Shane started to push inside. "Yeah, just like that. Just—"

Shane jerked awake with a gasp and lurched upright in bed. He wasn't in a limo, and he sure as hell wasn't having sex with Kayden Berlin. He was in his dark hotel room, alone. But his body was primed and ready to go, his erection a heavy weight between his legs.

Fuck.

Just another dream, same as all the others. It annoyed him to no end that he couldn't escape Kayden even in sleep. It was those damn eyes of his, so intensely green, so piercing. So beautiful. Was it any wonder that Shane couldn't stop thinking about them?

Ever since that shared limo ride back in Berlin, Shane had been dreaming about Kayden. About sucking him, fucking him, and whispering obscenities in his ear as he came. He even had a couple about Kayden topping him. In the shower, under the spray, with his face pressed up against the slick tile as Kayden used him. On a plane, right there in first class, with Kayden's fingers in his mouth to stop him from screaming as Kayden rode his body without mercy. The dreams were hot as hell, and they were driving him fucking *insane*.

Shane spent every night inundated by visions of himself and Kayden together. Then he woke up in the morning to face the reality that Kayden not only didn't want anything to do with him, he also saw Shane as a tired, stereotypical rock star who'd wasted his talent and never lived up to his full potential. It was a blow to the ego the likes of which he'd never experienced. And the worst part of it was that if it came from anyone other than Kayden, he probably wouldn't give a shit. But hearing it from Kayden—a musician he admired, someone whose respect he wanted so badly—it was a kick straight to the balls.

Shane sighed and settled back against the pillows. He had to be on a flight to Rome at the ass crack of dawn, and he was exhausted. But he knew there wasn't any way he was going to be able to fall asleep until he handled the raging hard-on tenting the sheets.

He reached over to the bed stand, grabbed the tube of lube lying there, and squirted a good amount into his palm. Thanks to the dreams, it had gotten to the point where he always kept some nearby. Aside from when he used it to get himself off, he hadn't needed the rather large stash of lube and condoms he packed into his suitcases prior to leaving the States.

Since that night with the twinks, before the tour had officially started, he hadn't brought anyone back to his room. Hard to think about anyone else when Kayden Berlin was in his face every day. Kayden, the walking wet dream. Kayden, who glowed so brightly, he made everyone else look beige and dull in comparison.

Had he ever wanted anyone even halfway as much as this? The only other person who came to mind was Jesse, but it had been different with Jesse, a slow-blooming desire as opposed to the lightning strike of lust that hit him the first time he saw Kayden in person.

Shane groaned and kicked the sheets off his legs. His dick was throbbing, almost painfully hard. He took it in hand, wrapped his fingers around the base, and started a languid stroke—up, a twist and squeeze at the head, then back down again. He pictured Kayden's face from the dream, that look of pleasure so intense, it bordered on pain. He thought of Kayden when he was onstage, every movement pure sex; Kayden's perfectly shaped mouth; his pale, pale hair; and the elegant eyebrows and thick lashes that showcased his eyes so well, several shades darker than that platinum blond. He remembered the glimpse he got of Kayden's masterpiece of an ass.

"Fuck."

Shane's strokes grew faster, rougher, his grip tightening. With his free hand, he cupped his sac, gently rolling his balls with his fingers. Sweat broke out over his skin, and his breathing quickened into shallow pants. He tugged and pulled at his lube-slick cock, flexing his hips as he thrust into his fist. The vision of Kayden arching beneath him, Kayden's fingernails digging into his back, spurred him on. Shane wanted to feel it all—Kayden's body under his, Kayden's legs wrapped around his waist or hoisted up over his shoulders, Kayden impaled on his dick. He wanted to kiss Kayden everywhere, to know every single inch of him. And after all that, he wanted Kayden against his side, wrapped around him while he fell asleep.

Shane shuddered, and the muscles in his thighs and lower abdomen tensed as his orgasm built. He jerked his fist a couple more times and came, his cock pulsing, cum spurting warm and slippery across his bare chest. Fingers still curled around his dick, he lay there for a few minutes afterward as his breath slowed and his limbs twitched sporadically.

When Shane had himself under control, he snagged a few tissues from the box on the nightstand and cleaned up. Going to the bathroom to do it would require way too much effort, and he could already feel sleep creeping over him in the aftermath of his orgasm. He tossed the used tissues aside, rolled onto his stomach, and cradled his head in his arms. Within seconds, he was out cold.

He didn't dream again.

SHANE SAT in one of the meeting rooms in the St. Regis Hotel, nursing a vodka tonic and quietly seething. He was surrounded by luxury, and a waiter hovered a few feet behind his chair, ready to cater to his every whim. But all he could see or think about was Kayden standing in the corner with Em, keeping their heads a bit too close together for Shane's liking. Em was giggling, and occasionally he swatted at Kayden's arm in his usual flirtatious way. And Kayden was grinning—*grinning*—at Luck's little manager, his expression open and playful. Shane had never been on the receiving end of one of those looks, and he resented the hell out of it.

Their managers had called an impromptu meeting for the members of Luck and Moonlight shortly after their arrival in Rome. Shane didn't care about the meeting. At that moment, all he wanted to know was why Kayden constantly shut down around him. There had to be more to it than the reason Kayden gave in the limousine. If Kayden had acted the same way to everyone in the band, Shane would have chalked it up to him being an asshole and put the guy from his mind. Maybe. But since that wasn't the case, Shane couldn't stop wondering *why*.

"Hey. You all right there, mate?"

Shane started at the sound of someone speaking directly to him. Surya stood beside his chair with an expectant look on his face. "Sorry. What was that?"

"Mind if I sit here?"

"No, of course not."

Surya pulled out one of the elegantly upholstered chairs and slumped into it with a sigh. "Man, you look as bad off as I feel. Bloody 5:00 a.m. flights." He signaled the waiter and ordered a whiskey neat. "Bit of the hair of the dog that bit me, eh? I was completely pissed last night. Didn't get back to the hotel until after three. H. just about ripped me a new one."

Shane chuckled, thinking of Moonlight's formidable manager, Heather. "Yeah, she's a little—"

"Terrifying," Surya finished with a laugh. He reached into his pocket and withdrew a pack of cigarettes. "She has this look that could shrivel a man's bollocks, I swear. Keeps us all in line, though." He shook out a cigarette, offering it to Shane. "Want one?"

"No, thanks."

Surya tossed the pack onto the table and lit his cigarette, leaning back in his chair as the waiter placed his drink in front of him. "So, anything you need to talk about?"

"Huh?"

"When I came in you were watching Kayden, and you looked rather...." Surya waved a hand. "Well, let's just say if looks could kill, mate."

Shane shrugged and stared down into his drink. He couldn't exactly discuss what was eating at him with one of Kayden's bandmates. Couldn't talk about it with Nicky either. Dre might have been an option, but there wasn't any guarantee he wouldn't just tell Nicky about it anyway, and Shane wasn't really in the mood to deal with his brother's shit-talking.

Surya continued, "Look, the thing you have to understand about Kayden is that he's a private sort of bloke. Doesn't talk much about himself, even to us. He's been that way for as long as I've known him."

Shane glanced sideways at Surya, trying not to look too interested but probably failing miserably. "How long is that?"

"Oh, some ten years." Surya sipped at his drink, his cigarette dangling from his fingers. "We met at uni."

Shane opened his mouth to ask another question, but a clap from the front of the room drew his attention. Em stood beside Heather near the windows. Kayden had joined Oliver at the other end of the table, close to where Nicky and the other members of Luck sat.

"Good morning, everyone," Em said. "We just have a little something to discuss with you all, and then you're free for the rest of the day." He turned to glance at Heather. "Did you want to do the honors?"

"Yes, thank you." Heather smiled. "There's a new night-club, Torrid, here in Rome, that just opened about a month ago. The owners know a few of the higher-ups at Hazard Records, and they've requested that a few members from both Luck and Moonlight put in an appearance at the club tonight. Surya and Oliver have already agreed to go, but we need some volunteers from Luck."

"It'll be good publicity," Em put in. "All your drinks and food will be on the house. And you'll only have to stay for an hour, though it *is* supposed to be the hottest club around, so I doubt you'll want to leave."

"Free booze?" Nick said. "Count us in. We'll shut that bitch down. Besides, it's been a while since I had some spaghetti sauce on my noodle."

Dre burst out laughing. Shane just sighed in exasperation.

"Spaghetti sauce on his noodle?" Surya wrinkled his forehead in confusion.

Shane shook his head. "Don't ask."

"Right."

"So...." Shane leaned closer to Surya, keeping his voice low. "Is Kayden not going tonight, then?"

Surya gave him a knowing look as he sucked a deep drag off his cigarette. "It's not really his cup of tea, yeah?" he said around an exhalation of smoke.

"Shane? Can we count you in for later?"

Shane glanced toward the front of the room to see both Em and Heather staring at him expectantly. "No, I think I'll just, um, hang around the hotel. Maybe go see some of the sights."

"What the hell for, lame-o?" Nick yelled from down the table. "What the fuck else is there to see other than some old-ass buildings?"

"Maybe I want some of my own spaghetti."

"Is this some sort of weird American thing?" Surya asked in a puzzled tone. "If you want spaghetti, you can just order room service, man."

Shane choked on a laugh. "This isn't that kind of hotel." He grinned at Surya, but the smile died when he noticed Kayden watching him with an expression of such intense scorn on his face, it made Shane's stomach clench.

Jesus, can't the guy take a joke?

"Okay." Em rubbed his hands together. "Then it'll be Dre, Nick, and Will from Luck, and Oliver and Surya from Moonlight. More than enough to meet our obligation. The cars will be here to pick you guys up at eight thirty. Until then, you're on your own, boys."

Shane finished his drink, said good-bye to Surya, and headed up to his room. He was probably deluding himself, but he had a plan. If he could get Kayden alone for a few hours, away from the prying eyes of their bandmates and managers, maybe Shane could break through to him, get him to open up a little. Unlikely as it was, it was worth a shot. Kayden wasn't immune to him, no matter what he tried to pretend, which meant there was a chance. No matter how slim it was, Shane wasn't about to let such a prime opportunity slip by.

CHAPTER FIVE

THIS IS SUCH A STUPID IDEA. HE'S NEVER GOING TO say yes.

Shane walked toward the door to Kayden's suite, trepidation building with every step. What had happened to the old badass version of Shane Ventura? The cocky bastard who never gave a shit about anything and could summon a groupie to his side with nothing more than a casual crook of his finger?

In the past, if a guy was hot, that was enough to satisfy Shane. He hadn't cared about personalities, religion, political views or anything else, because he never planned on getting involved with anyone beyond a quick suck and fuck in a random hotel room.

But for some reason he couldn't explain, he wanted more from Kayden. He wanted Kayden to actually *like* him, not because he was in a band, not because of his looks, but because somehow Kayden, a virtual stranger, saw past the rock star veneer to the person Shane was underneath.

And he wanted to give that to Kayden in return. He couldn't deny his physical attraction to Kayden—it would be a lie, and Christ knew he was desperate to get into the guy's pants—but in his many fantasies about Kayden, it never ended with just sex. He imagined falling asleep with Kayden, waking up with him, just *being* with him, playing music, sharing meals.

Truth be told, his feelings scared the hell out of him. He even freaked out about it in his room when he thought about the fact that he was going to ask Kayden on a date. A *date*, for fuck's sake. Shane had never actually been on one before. He couldn't count the times he'd gone out with Jesse, since they'd spent nearly every spare moment together anyway, and the subject had never come up. He and Jesse had never needed to define what they had. It was so easy, as simple as breathing. But their relationship ended before it really began. Probably for the best, considering what happened.

Shane stopped in front of Kayden's door, took a deep breath, and knocked. It seemed excessively loud in the silent hallway, and he cringed, hoping it hadn't sounded on Kayden's side like he was trying to pound the door down.

There was no answer for nearly a minute. As he waited, his heart beat in triple time and his palms grew damp with sweat. He'd just lifted his hand to knock again when the door swung inward, and Kayden stood there wearing an annoyed expression.

"Yes?"

Shane swallowed. "Hey, Kayden. I was just wondering, um, Have you eaten yet?"

Kayden gave him a strange look but shook his head after a few seconds. "No."

"Well, I haven't either, and I'm not really in the mood for room service. I was thinking... I'm here, you're here. Maybe we can go out for a late dinner or something?"

For a long moment, Kayden didn't answer, which Shane took as a good sign, since he'd expected him to refuse outright. Eventually Kayden shrugged. "All right."

"All right?" Shane repeated with a grin.

Kayden's eyes narrowed. "Yes. But just so we're clear, that's all this is."

Shane felt a twinge of disappointment, but he was too happy about the fact that Kayden had agreed to care about labels. "Of course. Just two guys going out for some food."

"Right. Well, I'll meet you down in the lobby in ten."

Shane nodded, knowing he probably looked like a total moron with how wide he was grinning, but he couldn't seem to help himself. "Okay."

"How did you find this place?" Kayden asked.

Shane glanced up from his menu. Not that he could read it, since it was entirely in Italian, but he'd hoped he would at least be able to recognize the name of an entrée or two. He searched Kayden's face for any signs of irritation but found none. In fact, Kayden looked more relaxed than Shane had ever seen him.

"I asked the concierge to recommend a mom-and-pop type of place. I didn't want anything too fancy."

"Good choice." Kayden picked up his own menu. His eyes moved over it quickly, and he laid it back down with a tiny smile playing about his lips. "My mother used to love coming to restaurants like this."

Shane stared, entranced by that sweet little smile. Finally, he found his voice. "You've been to Italy with your family?"

Kayden nodded. "We used to come on holiday every

summer while I was at uni. My parents owned a cottage on the outskirts of Tuscany."

"You're lucky." Shane thought back on his own childhood. "My family never really did much together. We only went on one vacation, and that was right before—" Shane broke off, not sure if he wanted to go there. It wasn't a very good memory.

"Right before?" Kayden prompted. His eyes were on Shane's face, and for the first time, he looked interested, as if he might actually care about what Shane had to say.

Under normal circumstances, Shane didn't like to talk about his past, especially not the more sordid details of growing up with a father like Angel Ventura. But right then, as Kayden regarded him with honest curiosity and none of his usual aloofness, he found himself wanting to share.

"Right before my mom left," Shane finished, setting his menu aside. "We went to visit her parents in Puerto Rico. They have a house outside of San Juan, in Levittown." He dropped his eyes to his place setting and reached out to rearrange his silverware according to height, just to give his hands something to do. "We went for Christmas break when I was in fourth grade. At first it was okay, but then my grandpa and my dad started arguing. My grandparents never liked him, and my grandpa just got sick of trying to play nice, I guess."

Shane abandoned the silverware and moved on to his water glass, tracing patterns in the condensation that had formed on the surface. He cleared his throat and continued.

"Anyway, one day they got into a really bad fight, and my dad took off. He showed up in the middle of the night and started yelling when he realized my grandparents had locked him out. My mom went outside to try to calm him down. Nicky and I watched her from the window, and I remember feeling so terrified, like something horrible was going to happen. And of course it did. When my mom unlocked the gate to let my dad in, he just started whaling on her. I saw her fall, and I didn't even think. I just ran out there." He stopped and gave a mirthless laugh. "I was only eight. I don't know what I thought I was gonna do, but I couldn't just stand there and let him hit her."

Shane risked a look at Kayden's face. The singer was watching him in silence, and there was something in his expression—empathy, maybe?—that made Shane's stomach clench. It was almost as if Kayden knew, or had guessed, how the story would end.

"So I ran out there like an idiot," Shane went on, determined to finish the story even if it was humiliating, "and I stood in front of her. I could smell the alcohol coming off him. I knew he was drunk. There was this thing he would say when he got like that. He'd give me a look, and he'd say, 'Are you eyeballing me, *boy?* You wanna fight me, *boy?*' Whenever he said that, Nicky and I knew we were about to get our asses kicked. Anyway, I don't remember much after that. He clocked me on the side of the head. Knocked me out. By the time I woke up, my grandparents had called the cops and my dad was gone. But my mom bailed him out the next morning, and he made us leave. That was the end of our family vacation."

Shane felt something brush across the top of his hand and looked down in surprise. Kayden's right hand was resting on his left, a soft, hesitant touch. Shane glanced back up at Kayden in shock.

Kayden wasn't looking at him, though. He was staring down at their hands, at his thumb, which was brushing soothingly over Shane's knuckles.

Shane held himself completely still, afraid that if he so

much as breathed, the moment would be broken. Kayden's fingers were toying with his, pale against the natural tan of Shane's skin. Eventually, the temptation grew too strong for Shane to resist. He lifted his hand and threaded their fingers together, squeezing lightly.

Almost immediately Kayden jerked away, as if he hadn't realized what he was doing until that moment. He looked flustered, his cheeks tinged pink with embarrassment. Then his mask, cool and remote, seemed to slip back into place, and the look was gone.

"I'm sorry," he said quietly. "That sounds awful."

Shane shrugged and tried to hide his frustration. For a few seconds, it had been the real Kayden sitting across from him, not the standoffish version he presented only to Shane and Nick. He wanted more of that Kayden, the one who touched him shyly and looked at him with understanding instead of derision.

Dammit.

Shane nearly sighed. Just when he thought he might be making some headway. He grabbed his menu again, scanned the unfamiliar text, and decided to change the subject.

"Can you read Italian? I don't see anything I recognize on this."

"I can read a bit," Kayden answered. "And I speak some Italian. Enough to get by in a pinch."

Shane looked up with a sheepish smile. "Help me pick something?"

Kayden arched a brow. "You like spicy?"

"Hell yeah."

"Then try the *penne all'arrabiata*. It has a lot of red pepper, but it's really good."

"I'll give it a shot. Is that what you're having?"

"I'm having gnocchi. With lots and lots of butter." Kayden smirked. "Might as well indulge. I love pasta, but I don't have it very often. Too many carbs."

"You don't look like you have to worry about that."

Kayden huffed and shook his head. "You *would* say something like that. You've probably never had to work to maintain that body of yours."

Shane was prevented from answering immediately by the arrival of their waiter. Kayden smiled at the guy and placed their order, his Italian sounding perfect as far as Shane could tell. When they were alone again, Kayden settled back in his seat and crossed his arms over his chest.

"Why does it always feel like I say the wrong thing to you?" Shane asked, perplexed. "I mean, am I that much of an asshole, or do you just choose to take everything I say the wrong way?"

Kayden shrugged. "I took it exactly the way you meant it. You look at me, you see a tight little body, and you can't think past that."

"I don't just see you as a body. I want to *know* you. I don't get why you won't give me a chance to do that."

"I'm giving you a chance. Right now."

"Then tell me about yourself. Tell me how Moonlight got together."

Kayden shifted in his chair, and for a moment, he looked uncomfortable. "It's not much of a story. I was in my third year at uni, and I saw a flyer about a band looking for a guitarist. I rang them up and we got together for a practice session. They asked me to join that same day, and a few years later we signed with Hazard."

Shane nodded, keeping his eyes focused on the table. Instinctively he reached up to toy with the shamrock that hung from the chain around his throat. Maybe he shouldn't have brought up the subject of how Moonlight hooked up. It made him think about Luck, and how they weren't even an official band until Jesse came into the picture—just a few punk kids messing around with shitty pawnshop instruments in his dad's basement. And he didn't want to think about Jesse, not with Kayden sitting across from him.

"I've been with Luck since high school," he said, just because it felt like he should say *something*.

Kayden didn't reply.

Worried he'd somehow said the wrong thing again, Shane glanced up. Kayden's gaze was focused on his hand, the one he was using to play with his chain. He looked... stunned. Shane released the shamrock self-consciously. "I wonder how long the food is going to take. I'm starving."

Shane's words seemed to snap Kayden out of his daze. He looked away, dropping his gaze to his wineglass. The fingers of his right hand had tightened around the stem, and his knuckles were white. Something was wrong, Shane could tell, but he had no idea what part of their conversation might have upset Kayden.

"So," he started, wanting to ease the sudden tension, "in Berlin you mentioned an ex. Is there...? Are you seeing someone right now?"

"No. Not at the moment."

"Why?" Shane asked automatically, then inwardly cursed himself for the tactless question.

Kayden gave a half shrug, but he didn't look up. "Relationships are difficult when you travel so much, as I'm sure you know. All of the time apart—he couldn't deal with it. He found someone else."

"His loss."

Kayden snorted. "I doubt he saw it that way." Finally,

he lifted his gaze from the wineglass and met Shane's. "What about you?"

"No. There's no one."

"I suppose that doesn't surprise me."

"What's that supposed to mean?"

"Let's just say you don't strike me as the boyfriend type." He looked at something over Shane's shoulder. "Ah, here comes our food."

Shane stayed silent as the server set down their plates with a cheerful "*Buon appetito.*"

Kayden smiled. "*Grazie.*"

The waiter said something else in Italian. From his tone it sounded like a question. Kayden replied and shook his head.

"Are you going to answer me?" Shane asked once the man had walked away.

Kayden sighed. "Let's just eat. I don't want to argue with you."

"Fine. Then tell me something else about yourself."

"Such as?" Kayden picked up his fork and dug into his pasta.

Tell me you want me as much as I want you. Shane wished he had the balls to say such a thing. He didn't want to risk Kayden freezing up on him. Or, worse, Kayden saying no, he didn't want anything to do with Shane, like before.

"I don't know. Anything."

"I want to go on a holiday," Kayden said between bites. "Somewhere nobody knows me, where I can just walk around, completely anonymous. No paparazzi, no fans, no managers. Just me."

"Wouldn't you be lonely?" Shane started on his own

food. The penne was delicious, with enough of a kick to leave a pleasant heat on his tongue.

"Not at all. I think the value of solitude is vastly under-rated. Don't you ever just want to be by yourself?"

"Sometimes, I guess." Shane shrugged. "But when I'm alone, I think too much."

"That's not necessarily a bad thing. Perhaps you could use some self-reflection."

Shane didn't think so. Not when, aside from Kayden, both his waking and sleeping thoughts revolved around how tired he was and how meaningless everything seemed. No amount of self-reflection could help with that because it always, *always* came back to Jesse.

Nothing had been able to fill the void since Shane lost his best friend. So he kept throwing things at it, hoping one day, something would stick. And nothing ever came close. Except now, when Shane looked at Kayden, a part of him just *knew*. If Kayden let him in, let him get close, they could have something. Something amazing. He could feel it, even if he couldn't explain it. Kayden was that missing piece.

Aside from a bit of chitchat about how the tour was going so far, they finished their food mostly in silence. Unlike their usual encounters, it wasn't awkward. It was comfortable, easy. Shane paid for the meal, brushing aside Kayden's protests, and they exited the restaurant into the balmy night.

It was late, but the streets were still crowded. Shane glanced at Kayden. He didn't want their time together to end, and he knew if they went back to the hotel, it would be over. "Do you want to go for a walk? Look around a little?"

"Sure," Kayden replied, surprising him. "It'll be a while before I can come back here. I wouldn't mind seeing Trevi Fountain again. We're not too far."

"That's cool. Lead the way."

Kayden turned right and started weaving through the crowd. Shane took a moment to admire the view—Kayden was wearing a pair of tight black pants that left next to nothing to the imagination—and then rushed to catch up with him.

They'd been walking for only a few minutes when a bolt of lightning clawed its way across the sky, followed by a rumble of thunder so loud it made Shane cringe.

"Well, that seems rather ominous." Kayden's chuckle sounded nervous. "Maybe we should skip the fountain and go back to the hotel."

Disappointment sliced through Shane's belly. It was just his luck that the weather would turn to shit the one time Kayden seemed agreeable, even friendly toward him. He didn't imagine there'd be very many opportunities for them to be totally alone in the near future, considering the fact that the final concert of the European portion of the tour was only a couple of days away and they'd be on hiatus for three weeks after that. Besides, who was to say that Kayden would ever give him another chance anyway?

"Yeah, all right," he said when Kayden looked over at him. His words were punctuated by another boom of thunder.

"Come on. If I'm remembering right, we can cut down this street to get back to Via Rasella. It shouldn't be too complicated from there."

Shane didn't have a clue where they were. He nodded and followed Kayden. Darkness thickened around them as they moved farther down the narrow side street. There was another clap of thunder, and then it was as if someone turned on a faucet overhead. Rain poured down in heavy torrents, and within seconds, they were drenched to the skin.

"Shit!" Shane grabbed Kayden's arm and pulled him under the archway of the building they were walking past. At the ground level it was a small café, already closed and locked up for the night. A light fixture glowed above the door, illuminating the entryway. It wasn't very bright, but at least it was something. "Holy fuck. That came out of nowhere."

"Yeah, you think?" Kayden's voice was amused, but Shane didn't miss the slight tremor underneath. "Not even a drop of warning."

Shane stared out into the street. The rainfall was so dense, he couldn't see through it. The water hit the pavement with loud, heavy splats.

"This reminds me of that time I got drunk in Vegas," Shane said, trying to alleviate some of the tension. He paused. "Well, one of the times. Anyway, I got totally wasted and passed out the moment I got back from the bar. I started dreaming that I was caught out in a thunderstorm, and I nearly pissed myself right there in bed. I woke up at the last moment and hauled ass to the bathroom. Must've pissed for five minutes straight. It sounded kind of like this."

Kayden burst out laughing. Shocked, Shane turned to look at him. Fuck, even the guy's laugh was adorable. Shane had never particularly paid attention to anyone's laugh before, not unless it was weird or irritating. But like everything else about Kayden, that breathy laugh turned Shane on. And the tiny little snorting sound he made halfway through was totally endearing.

Kayden caught Shane watching him and abruptly stopped laughing. He covered his mouth with his hand, and Shane could see he was blushing in the dim light.

"Don't hide." Shane didn't even stop to think about what he was doing. He took Kayden's hand and moved it aside, then used his other hand to cup Kayden's cheek. "You're beautiful."

And he was. Beautiful beyond words. He had such a gorgeous mouth, perfectly shaped, with just a hint of a pout. It drove Shane crazy. He brushed his thumb across Kayden's lower lip and leaned closer. Their mouths were only centimeters apart, and for one crazy, pulse-pounding second, he thought Kayden would actually allow the kiss. Maybe even return it. Then he felt a hand on his chest.

"No," Kayden said without meeting Shane's eyes. "Don't ruin it."

Shane released Kayden's hand and stepped back. His throat ached, but he tried to brush the hurt away. Kayden was right. Too much, too soon. Whatever he and Kayden had, it wouldn't survive if Shane tried to rush things. Logically, he knew that. But after having come so close to finally being able to touch, to taste, the rejection stung.

"It looks like it's died down a bit." Kayden left the cover of the archway and peered up at the sky. "If we hurry, maybe we can make it to the hotel before it starts again."

"Let's go, then."

By the time they made it back to the St. Regis, there wasn't an inch on Shane's body that wasn't soaking wet. He and Kayden nodded at the security guards who were posted at the doors and crossed the hotel's elegant lobby, tracking water across the marble. Shane cringed at the squeaky noises coming from his water-logged boots.

A man and woman were stepping out of one of the elevators just as Kayden and Shane arrived. The couple edged around them, eyeing them oddly and murmuring to each other. Under normal circumstances, Shane might have been amused. But as it was, he was cold and uncomfortable, trapped somewhere between misery and elation. He'd gotten more from Kayden than he expected, and that made him happy. But the night hadn't ended quite the way he hoped.

Shane boarded the elevator and hit the button for Kayden's floor.

"What level are you on?" Kayden asked when Shane made no move to hit any other numbers.

"The fourth." Shane reached up to brush sopping wet hair out of his face. He'd probably have to wring out his clothes when he got back to his suite. Goddamn rain.

"Shouldn't you be getting off, then?"

Shane glanced over at Kayden. His light-blue shirt clung to his skin, and his nipples were hard, clearly visible through the saturated material. Shane bit back a groan and forced himself to look away. "I wanted to walk you to your room."

"That's not necessary."

"I want to."

"Suit yourself."

The elevator dinged, and the doors slid open. Shane followed Kayden out and trailed him down the hall to his suite. Once there, Kayden withdrew his key card and slid it into the lock. "Thanks for dinner," he said over his shoulder.

"Kayden?" Shane reached out to touch his arm. Kayden stilled with a hand on the doorknob. "I had a good time tonight."

Kayden didn't answer for a long moment. Then Shane saw him nod, and he spoke so quietly Shane had to strain to hear the words. "Me too."

"Can we do it again sometime?"

Another long beat of silence. "Maybe."

Kayden disappeared into his room without saying anything else or looking back. It should've bothered Shane, but instead he found himself smiling. He walked back toward the elevators with a grin on his face, oblivious to his chafing jeans and waterlogged boots. He'd gotten through to Kayden; he was sure of it. He'd gotten under Kayden's skin.

CHAPTER SIX

Then....
Chicago

"Can you believe that guy chucked a beer bottle at Nick last night?" Jesse asked with a laugh. He covered his mouth like he always had, even though the embarrassing braces had come off over a year ago.

Jesse was lying on his stomach on his bed, legs bent at the knees, twirling a pencil around in his hand. Occasionally he paused to make a random note in the notebook that rested on the mattress between his elbows.

Shane chuckled at the memory of his brother's stunned face and strummed a few chords on Jesse's acoustic. He was sitting cross-legged on the carpet, and he craned his neck to look up at Jesse.

"Nicky shouldn't have yelled 'fuck off' at him."

Jesse smiled, but he tucked his head down and to the side. Shane knew they were going to have to work on the self-esteem issues if Jesse wanted to be a rock god.

"I can see why he did it, though. That guy was being a total asshole."

Shane nodded. Jesse was right. He'd been heckling them ridiculously, not even listening to their intro chords before yelling "you suck!"

"Guess we won't be playing at that bar again," Shane muttered with a sigh.

"No, we are. Next Wednesday. The owner said some of the regulars are already asking about us. He asked me to control Nick, though."

Shane snorted. "I can barely control him, and he's my brother."

"True." Jesse nodded with a shrug and went back to scribbling in his notebook.

Shane strummed a few more chords on Jesse's acoustic, his mind on the past few months. The local bar scene was brutal. None of them were even old enough to be in most of the venues they played, and they were rarely allowed to leave the stage area for anything other than to use the restroom. The audiences were usually about a half step above blatantly rude, and some, like the previous night's, were just plain awful.

But he knew Luck had to pay their dues. They'd started after a few months' practice, playing cover tracks for the school dance and bar mitzvah scene. That sucked, and the pay was terrible. Shane and Jesse worked the whole time, writing their own material and making call after call, trying to break into something real. They played a few open mic nights and got the attention of a local booker, who signed them up at most of the places they were currently playing.

In the two years the band had been together, they got so much better, meshing well with each other and getting tighter with every performance. They had to work around Jesse's college classes and Nick's school schedule.

There was no way Shane was going to let his little brother drop out, no matter how many times he begged, and Jesse... well, he would never even consider it. But Shane knew Jesse thought it was worth it sometimes to stumble into class tired as hell if they happened to get a good weekday gig. Shane hoped upon hope that someday soon their gigs would be stadiums and not seedy bars.

Shane had even been working on Jesse a little bit. He convinced him to lose the bowl cut for a bit of a punky spike and talked him into a stylish (and much smaller) pair of glasses. The pleated khakis Jesse wore in high school had long since been replaced by jeans, which were a vast improvement. There wasn't much Shane could do about... well, about the rest of it. But he didn't see it so much anymore. He saw pretty gray eyes, nice skin, and soft-looking lips, and there was that voice, which still managed to give him the chills.

Aw, shit... am I into him?

No. Not Jesse. Not his nerdy, pudgy best friend. Shane had been dating. Well, not dating, but screwing around. It was surprisingly easy to find random bar hookups, even if you were in an underage no-name band that played every Friday night for free beer and tips. But he'd been feeling lately like something was missing.

That couldn't be it. Could it?

Jesse's breath caught in his throat. *Breathe... breathe.* It was just Shane. It was always just Shane. Problem was, Shane hadn't ever been "just" anything. He started off as the most intimidating guy Jesse had ever met, turned into his first real friend, and then... well, then there was the pathetic crush he'd had on Shane since practically forever. Yeah. "Just Shane" was bullshit.

Shane was everything to him. He had been all along. Jesse knew Shane loved him too. But not like that. Never like that.

He stared at his notebook, feeling awkward around his best friend for the first time since they were sitting in the library together the day they met—Shane sullen and angry, Jesse terrified as hell. *That* awkward was nothing like this one. Back then it had been a whole lot of "please don't stab me with your pen" mixed in with a little "damn, he'd be hot if he wasn't such an asshole." Not anymore. Now it was that moment, the place where Jesse didn't think he could spend another two years waiting to tell Shane how he felt. He knew, hell it was obvious, that he and Shane could never be, but the longer he kept it inside, the weirder he'd start to act. He was never good at keeping secrets. Jesse cleared his throat. Shane craned his neck to look up at him.

"What's up, man?"

Talk, moron. Say something.

"Hey, listen to this." He twisted around so he was leaning forward halfway off the bed with his notebook on the floor. "I thought it would be cool if we had an acoustic track, something pretty."

"Yeah? Let's hear it." Shane smiled at him, and Jesse tried not to choke on his own dumb emotions. What made him think *singing* was a good idea?

"Start with a B minor chord, then switch to a G." Jesse pulled Shane's hand into position on the guitar's fret board.

He really wasn't using the music as an excuse to touch Shane's hand. That would be unfair to music, and Jesse loved music, right? Shane knew damn well what a B minor and G chord looked like on his guitar, too, but still Jesse brushed their fingers together as he lifted his hand away when Shane began to play.

"Yeah, do it again, just like that. Play it in three."

Jesse started to sing and hoped like hell his voice didn't crack. Everything he had was in these damn lyrics, his chest pulled open so Shane and whoever else was listening could see every sad little hope in his heart. He figured he might as well tell Shane. It wasn't like everyone in the whole universe wasn't blinded by his obvious adoration anyway.

"*Second glances,*
warmed from the sun,
moments slow passing,
never done."

Shane's eyes widened and went kind of soft. "Jess, that's gorgeous." Jesse tried not to let himself believe he meant anything more than the song. "Nothing like our usual stuff. You got any more?" Shane's voice cracked just a little bit. Jesse held his breath.

I love you. I've loved you for years.

Jesse coughed. "I'm, um, having trouble with this next part." He grabbed his notebook and showed Shane the place where he'd been erasing and scratching lines out all afternoon.

Shane studied the page Jesse pointed out. He'd scooted up a bit so their faces were right there, their cheeks sharing warmth through the nearly nonexistent space between them. It felt like they were touching. Like the heated, charged air connected them somehow, arced between them, drew them closer. Jesse shivered. He couldn't help it.

"So, *For the first time...?*"

"Y-yeah, and then I'm lost after that."

Heat, heartbeat, smooth lips, soft hair, so close, want him closer.... Play it cool. We're just writing a damn song.

"How 'bout *Someone sees who I am?*"

"*And I can't let you... slip through my hands.*" Jesse finished the verse in a whisper, turning his face toward Shane. Shane leaned forward just a touch. Was Shane really going to? No. No way. He leaned forward himself. Shane didn't back away. Was he? Jesse's whole body pulsed with his racing heartbeat.

Ohgodohgodohgod....

What the hell?

Shane wanted to.... He was going to.... Jesse's mouth got closer. Shane could feel the heat from Jesse's breath radiating across his face. He couldn't believe it—he wanted to kiss Jesse.... *Jesse.* And Jesse wanted to kiss him back.

Shane reached up and skimmed his thumb across a peachy cheek tanned from the late-spring sun. Their lips were brushing, barely touching, and then Jesse curled his hand around Shane's neck and kissed him. Really kissed him. It was *amazing.* Shane didn't have room to think, almost forgot to breathe. All he could do was feel Jesse's lips on his, soft and eager, pure and sweet, exactly what he hadn't known he wanted. And it made perfect sense.

"*Shane,*" Jesse whispered against his lips.

The whisper gave him goose bumps, just like Jesse's singing voice. He reacted instinctively, cupping the back of Jesse's head with his hand and pulling him closer, closer, as close as he could get. Shane opened his lips to taste Jesse and—

The knock on Jesse's door was loud, jarring them from their quietly life-changing moment.

"Jesse, dinner's ready."

Shane dropped Jesse's guitar from his lap with a clatter and pulled his hand away from Jesse's neck as if his skin had suddenly burst into flames. He felt like Jesse's mother could see everything they'd been doing on the other side of that innocent-looking door. His face burned.

"Shane, honey, you can stay too if you want."

"Thanks, Mrs. Seider."

Shane was trembling and a bit freaked out. He stood and righted Jesse's guitar on its stand. "Uh, so, that's all you have so far. For the song?"

"Yeah," Jesse said. "I'll work on it and, um, maybe we can practice it another day. You staying for dinner?"

Shane shook his head. "I should probably get home and check on Nicky. Dad's been on a bender lately."

Jesse cringed. "You know, you guys can come here if you need to."

Shane huffed out a small chuckle. "What would your parents think of Nicky? He's kind of...."

"He's kind of Nicky. I know. So, I'll talk to you later?" Jesse looked at Shane, hopeful, confused. Everything Shane was feeling was written all over Jesse's face.

Shane found himself grinning. Then he leaned over and gave Jesse one more small kiss on the lips, just so Jesse knew how it was between them.

"Yeah. I'll talk to you later."

Shane hardly felt the stairs under his feet, but he must have walked down them because before he knew it, he was out on the street and heading for the bus stop. His head was spinning, but he wanted to do cartwheels and laugh and freak the hell out all at the same time.

He couldn't believe he'd been so blind—that all the stomach flips, the warm feelings, the way he wanted to be around Jesse all the time, the way Jesse had gravitated toward him whenever they were in the same room, hadn't come together in his head before. Maybe he hadn't wanted them to. It didn't matter. He wasn't clueless anymore. Everything he'd been feeling for months made perfectly clear sense. Finally.

Shane was in love.

Now....
Barcelona

SHANE COULDN'T QUITE BELIEVE it when he knocked on Kayden's door the morning after they arrived in Barcelona and actually got an answer. Most of the guys had gone out and partied the night before. It was early enough that the halls in the hotel were empty and quiet, but Shane hadn't been able to stay in his room for even a second longer.

He'd been waiting for another opportunity to get Kayden alone since their dinner in Rome. Now that the three-week break between the European and American legs of the tour was about to begin, he couldn't afford to wait anymore. It was go to Kayden now or lose his chance for nearly a month. Shane was too desperate to let the threat of rejection put him off. So he went.

Kayden eyed him for a long moment. His hair was damp, and from the fresh, clean smell of his skin, Shane could tell he'd probably just gotten out of the shower. The thought of Kayden slick and wet almost made him groan. He forced the mental image away as Kayden arched an imperious brow. "Yes?"

Shane didn't let Kayden's frosty greeting discourage him. He grinned. "Morning. You had breakfast yet?"

Kayden crossed his arms over his chest, not looking at all encouraging. After a second, he shook his head. "No."

"Well, you're awake... and I'm obviously awake."

"Obviously." Kayden's lips quirked at the corners, a hint of a smile, quickly smothered. "Is this the way you ask everyone out?"

Shane's grin widened. "I was doing my best not to make it sound like a date. Didn't want to scare you off."

Kayden shook his head, but Shane saw a glimpse of a smile as he turned away. "Give me a minute."

A minute turned into five as Kayden disappeared into the bedroom and left Shane fidgeting in the sitting area. When he came back, his hair was slicked forward and the loose, soft T-shirt he'd been wearing exchanged for a deep purple V-neck that molded to his chest as if it had been poured on.

Shane did his best not to drool as they left the suite. After a short discussion while waiting for the elevator, they opted for the restaurant on the second floor of the hotel instead of trying to find a different one nearby.

A number of startled looks and a wave of excited whispering followed in their wake as they walked into the restaurant. By now, everyone in the hotel had probably heard they were staying there, but no one bothered them as they were quickly escorted to a small, relatively private table away from the main eating area.

Kayden settled in to the seat across from Shane and picked up his menu. Shane tried not to stare, but the sunlight pouring in from the window beside their table only made Kayden more beautiful. His hair shone, so pale a blond that at a quick glance, it could be mistaken for white. His eyes were greener than ever, and his skin looked as silky as the finest cream. Shane knew that skin was just as soft to the touch as it appeared. He only wished he could get his hands on more of it.

"Do you know what you want?" Kayden asked suddenly.

Shane started in his chair. "Pancakes," he said without thinking.

Kayden smirked. "I don't think that's an option."

"Oh." Shane finally tore his gaze away from Kayden and looked at the small menu in front of him. Kayden was right, of course. He saw a variety of things on the menu—sweet rolls, tortilla, and what sounded a lot like French toast—but nothing like the typical pancake breakfast combo he might order back home.

"Um," he said after a moment. "I guess the bread things. The *torrijas*. And coffee."

"That sounds good. I think I'll have an omelet and some fruit." Kayden lifted his hand and waved for the waiter who hovered nearby. Once the orders were placed and their menus collected, he sat back and sipped at the glass of water the server had dropped off.

"Are you nervous about tonight?" Shane asked when the silence got to be too much. "Last concert before the break and all."

Kayden shrugged. "I get a little nervous every time. I don't think I'll ever be jaded enough not to be. There are a thousand and one things that can go wrong. I want people to get their money's worth."

Shane nodded. "I hear that."

"What about you? Do you still get nervous?"

"Sometimes."

Shane wanted to say more, like how before this tour he'd been to the point where his entire career felt meaningless, and it was hard to scrounge up the enthusiasm to get anxious about a concert. But the last time he mentioned something similar, Kayden had gotten pissed off and walked away. Shane would do anything not to have a repeat of that incident on the balcony in London. He changed the subject.

"Any plans for the rest of the day?" They were free until sound checks later, and those wouldn't be until the evening.

"Nothing really. I might hit the gym or work on some lyrics."

"Maybe we could do something together."

Kayden looked at Shane for a long moment before dropping his gaze to his silverware. "I don't think so."

Shane's stomach dropped. "Why?"

"I'd just rather not."

Shane sighed and raked a hand through his hair. God, with all the frustrated yanking he'd been doing to it lately, he might be bald by the time the tour was over. "What is it with the back and forth shit with you? I mean, in Rome it seemed like we might be cool."

Kayden met his eyes. "You push too hard."

"I... I just want to.... It's gonna be three weeks before—"

"Don't. Can we not argue? Can we just talk and enjoy our meal and leave it at that?"

Shane swallowed down everything he wished he could say—that they wouldn't be arguing at all if Kayden just gave him half a chance—and forced himself to nod instead. "Talk to me, then. I feel like I barely know anything about you."

Kayden turned his gaze to the window beside them. "There isn't much to know. I write lyrics, I make albums, I perform. That's my entire life summed up in a sentence."

"But what else do you like to *do*? Outside of music."

"I read. When I have the time, I shop for antiques. Sometimes I just drink tea and enjoy being at home and the fact that I don't have anything *to* do. I love the travel and excitement of touring, but there are times I just like to stay still for a while. Try to see my family and friends, and when I have a boyfriend, spend time with him. Just be as normal as I can be."

Shane's jaw clenched at the mention of a boyfriend. Even a nonexistent one. *Jesus Christ, what is my problem?* Shane had never been the jealous type; then again, he'd never really dated either. Aside from Jesse. Since Jesse there had been nothing but threesomes, moresomes, and way too many one-night stands. Jealousy didn't have the ground in which to take root when he never saw the same guy for more than a night.

He pushed thoughts of Kayden's exes from his head and focused on the rest of what Kayden said.

"I understand what you mean." And he did. The constant travel really could be exhausting. As a kid, he'd never have guessed the rock star lifestyle would ever get old. But it had. Before Moonlight and Kayden Berlin. "Sometimes I think about taking a break, but I don't know what I'd do with myself if I wasn't making music."

Kayden chuckled softly. "Same here. It's in my blood."

Shane opened his mouth to ask if Kayden meant that literally or figuratively—maybe his parents were musicians too—but their server arrived then to deliver their order. Shane sat back as plates of steaming hot food and mugs of coffee were set on the table.

Kayden dug into his food without another word, and Shane started on his own instead of trying to press for more conversation. Once again, the silence between them was comfortable, but the underlying current of tension didn't fade entirely. Shane guessed it probably never would unless they fucked each other senseless. Maybe not even then, though Shane was willing to give it his best effort. But those thoughts were better left for a time when he wasn't sitting in an increasingly crowded restaurant. So he kept his attention on the cinnamon-and-sugar flavored bread on his plate and simply relaxed in the company of the man he wished he could spend every minute with.

Maybe someday soon he could find out if they'd be as explosive in bed together as he imagined.

KAYDEN WAS on his fourth shot. Shane was counting. He sat on a plush lounge chair on the terrace of their Barcelona hotel, a rum and Coke forgotten in his hand. The night was hot, thick with humidity, and the hotel stood close enough to the beach that Shane could smell the tang of salt in the air.

He ignored the heat, the party that raged around him, and the inviting glances the sexy Spanish bartender kept casting in his direction. His eyes were locked on Kayden, had been since the singer finally deigned to make an appearance at the celebratory soiree Hazard Records was hosting to mark the end of the European leg of the Lucky Moon Tour.

Three months of travel had finally drawn to a close with their concert earlier that evening. The following morning would start the three-week break before they reunited in Chicago to kick off the US leg of the tour. That meant almost a month without seeing Kayden, hearing his voice, or watching him perform. After Rome and their breakfast that morning, those weeks seemed to stretch out like a lifetime.

Despite what Kayden said earlier, Shane had hoped they might be able to spend a little more time together during the day before the concert. But Kayden had gone back up to his suite after their meal, and from that point on, seemed to go out of his way to avoid Shane.

He walked into a room, and suddenly Kayden found an excuse to leave. He tried to speak as they passed each other, but Kayden avoided his eyes and kept walking. Then, after the concert, Shane tried going up to Kayden's suite, but his knock went unanswered. In fact, Kayden didn't show his face again until the after-party was in full swing.

Shane spotted him the second he stepped out onto the terrace—Shane and just about everyone else who was there. But Kayden didn't even look his way. He went over to talk to his bandmates for a few minutes, and then Em approached and drew him over to a lounge chair near the pool. Shortly after that, the shots had started, and the space between Em and Kayden narrowed until Shane's tiny manager was practically in the singer's lap with his mouth up to Kayden's ear, and all Shane wanted to do was run over there, toss Em aside, and take his place.

Instead, he sat and fumed, watching the minutes tick away on his watch, his jealousy a vise that tightened around his stomach until he thought he might be sick. Why did Kayden have this sort of power over him when they'd barely even touched? Shane had no real right to be jealous. But just the thought of Kayden being with someone else, kissing someone else, whether it was Em or one of the hot little twinks who sat at the bar, made Shane want to commit physical violence.

It was extreme, and it was unsettling, but Shane couldn't help it any more than he could stop the sun from rising. It simply *was*. He couldn't understand it; at that moment, he didn't feel inclined to try too hard. All he knew was the night was drawing to a close and it would only be a matter of hours before they all went their separate ways.

Desperation pulsed in his veins with every beat of his heart, a craving for just one more hit, a few more minutes in Kayden's company. He *needed* it.

Shane couldn't stop thinking about their time in Rome, the feel of Kayden's hand on his, their fingers entwined, the almost kiss. He'd dreamed about it, that moment in the doorway of that café when Kayden laughed, open and honest, and Shane got so, *so* close to finally knowing the taste of him. He'd fantasized that the kiss had actually happened, that he kissed Kayden senseless, breathless, until Kayden melted against him and let Shane fuck him, right there under that archway, with the rain as their privacy curtain.

When Em laughed loudly and flung his arm around Kayden for a quick hug, Shane gripped his glass so tightly, he heard it creak. He decided to set the damn thing down before it shattered in his hand. That would be all he needed, a trip to a Spanish emergency room, to put the cherry on top of the shitastic sundae his night had become.

A waiter stopped by with a fifth round of shots for Em and Kayden. Shane's eyebrows shot up. He'd never seen Kayden drink more than a glass of wine, yet there he was, downing shots like water as he smiled and laughed with Em. And Shane would bet it was that same low, breathy laugh that made his cock twitch.

After Em had drained his shot glass, he gave Kayden another hug, planted a quick kiss on his cheek, and bounced off to mingle with some of the execs from Hazard. His normally animated hand gestures were even more pronounced than usual.

Shane suspected his manager was drunk. *Really* drunk. It wasn't something that happened very often—Shane could only remember maybe a handful of times in the eleven-plus years Em had managed Luck—and for a moment, he could only stare after Em in bemusement. But then out of the corner of his eye he saw Kayden stand up, saw him stumble, and all thoughts of Em fled.

He watched as Kayden left the terrace, heading away from the hotel instead of toward it. There were two walkways on that side. One path led deeper into the city and the other toward the beach. Shane could guess what direction Kayden would take, but it took him so long to fight his way through the crowd that Kayden had already disappeared by the time he reached the end of the terrace.

Shane waved back the security guard that made to follow him and peered up and down the street. His saving grace was the gleam of Kayden's pale hair under one of the lampposts in the distance, which told Shane he was correct in his assumption that Kayden would choose the lure of the Mediterranean over all the concrete, steel, and glass the rest of the city had to offer.

He followed in the direction Kayden had gone with quick steps. Kayden was moving slowly. He occasionally stopped and appeared to sway a bit, and his halting progress allowed Shane to catch up with him at the edge of the sand.

"Kayden? Where are you going?"

Kayden paused and glanced over his shoulder. It was darker near the beach, away from the glow of the streetlights. Shane couldn't read Kayden's expression, but he sounded amused. "Stalking me again?"

"Not stalking." Okay, *maybe* he was stalking. "I just wanted to talk to you. I know you've been avoiding me."

Kayden shrugged and stepped out onto the sand. "We talked this morning. What else is there to talk about?"

"Em, for starters."

Kayden laughed and kept moving unsteadily toward the water. "What about him?"

Shane followed. "Is something going on between you two? Are you into him or something?"

Kayden snorted and giggled. *Giggled.* Shane's eyes widened. *Holy hell, just how drunk is he?*

"What business is it of yours?" Kayden asked, looking back at Shane over his shoulder.

At that precise instant, he tripped, apparently on thin air, and would have gone face-first into the sand if Shane hadn't grabbed his arm. "Jesus, you're a lightweight, aren't you? No wonder I never see you drink."

Kayden jerked away and lifted his chin. "I'm not a lightweight. I just haven't eaten since breakfast."

"Uh-huh."

Kayden huffed as he turned back toward the water. The sound of the surf was calming as the waves licked over the shore and retreated in a steady rhythm. A marina sat to the left, where dozens of moored sailboats bobbed and shone in the moonlight, and before them the sea stretched darkly toward the horizon.

"It's beautiful here," Kayden said suddenly, startling Shane. "I love the smell of saltwater."

Shane nodded. "It reminds me of being in Puerto Rico. My grandparents' house isn't very far from the water."

"Have you been back since that time?"

The question surprised Shane, but he answered with a shrug, "Yeah. We've played a few concerts in San Juan."

"No. I meant to see your grandparents."

Shane tensed. He was tempted to visit them the first time Luck played in San Juan, but he suspected when his mother abandoned him and Nicky, she returned to her parents on the island, and he couldn't risk seeing her. Not after she left him and his brother in the care of their douche bag of a father without a backward glance or a single phone call in all the years that followed.

"No," he finally answered.

Kayden nodded and stayed quiet for a few seconds. When he spoke again, his voice was contemplative. "There's nothing going on between Em and me, by the way. We're just friends." He glanced sideways at Shane. "You might want to try that sometime."

"I am try—"

"Besides"—Kayden went on as if Shane hadn't spoken —"my name isn't Surya, and that's what Em and I talk about most of the time anyway."

Shane blinked. "Surya?"

Kayden laughed. "I know. Unlikely pair, that." He reached up to brush his bangs off his forehead. "Christ, why is it so hot? It's the middle of the night. Maybe I should go for a swim."

He went for the water, fully dressed, shoes and all. Shane snagged his wrist in alarm. "I don't think that's such a smart idea."

Kayden stumbled and crashed against his chest. He peered up at Shane, close enough that Shane could have leaned forward just a fraction and sealed their mouths together.

"You know," Kayden said, his warm breath radiating over Shane's skin, "I've always loved your eyes. You look good in eyeliner."

Shane stared down at him in shock, his grip on Kayden's wrist loosening. "What?"

"I'm going for a swim." Kayden pulled away from Shane with so much force, he flew backward and landed on his ass in the wet sand. He sat there for a moment, looking stunned, then burst out laughing and let himself fall back. A wave crawled up the shore and over the right half of his lower body, drenching his clothes. "The great Shane Ventura," he mumbled as he fisted a handful of sand. "Who would've ever guessed?"

Shane leaned over him. "Shit, how drunk are you?"

"What? I'm allowed to be a rock star too, aren't I?" Kayden smirked. "Though, admittedly, you do corner the market on drunken debauchery, don't you?"

"Come on." Shane knelt down and reached for Kayden's arm. "I'll take you back to the hotel."

Kayden's only response was to fling a glob of wet, gritty sand at Shane's shirt. It landed with a squelch, spattering across the dark material. He laughed and started gathering another handful. "Not so tough now, are you?"

Shane gaped at him but came to his senses before Kayden could throw another clump of sand. He dove across Kayden's body to pin his arm, and they grappled for a few moments, Kayden laughing all the while. It occurred to Shane too late that he was getting more sand on himself by wrestling around with Kayden in the surf than if he would have just dodged Kayden's throw or if Kayden had managed to hit him again. On top of that, his clothes were getting soaked, and he had water in his boots again.

But the plus side was that Kayden was writhing beneath him, and it felt good. So good that Shane's cock began to respond and made its presence known against Kayden's hip.

Kayden went still under him. He looked up at Shane, but the shadows made his face unreadable. "Why does it seem like I always wind up wet whenever we're alone together?"

Shane grinned. "What can I say? It's a gift."

Kayden chuckled, the sound low and dark. Shane

nudged his hips forward and felt Kayden's answering erection through the sodden layers of their clothing. "And now you're hard too." He leaned down and brushed his lips against Kayden's as he spoke. "Want me to do something about that for you?"

Kayden turned his head, stopping the kiss before it could begin. But he moved under Shane, parting his legs to accommodate Shane's hips and grinding their pelvises together. Shane groaned softly, disappointed that Kayden had denied him yet another kiss, but he wasn't about to complain. He pressed his mouth to Kayden's pale white throat instead, nipping and sucking in turn, as he ground down and Kayden thrust up.

He forgot about the fact that they were on a public beach, that they'd probably be arrested for public indecency or something if the cops showed up and found them that way. And Lord only knew what the media fallout would be if some enterprising paparazzo snapped a picture of them dry humping each other in the sand.

But how could he think about any of that with Kayden beneath him, Kayden's cock rubbing against his? He imagined he could feel the heat of it, even through the material that separated them, and the very idea made his dick harden even further.

They fell into an easy rhythm, rising and falling, their breaths quickening. Kayden slid his hands beneath Shane's shirt, his palms gritty with wet sand, but Shane liked the feel of it, rough against the smooth skin of his back. Waves ebbed and flowed over them as they moved, but he was oblivious to the chill of the water. All he could feel, see, think about was Kayden. He dropped frantic kisses across Kayden's neck, his collarbones, his jaw, and moved his hips faster and faster, his breathing ragged.

Kayden was making noises that made Shane's dick throb, soft little moans right next to his ear. If he wasn't careful, those sounds alone would make him come. He tried to pull back, tried to slow down. He didn't know if or when something like this would happen again, and he wanted it to *last*.

"God, you feel so good." Shane buried his face against Kayden's throat and slipped a hand between their bodies. He rubbed his palm over Kayden's length, wishing the pants were gone so he could wrap his fingers around that rigid, satiny flesh.

Kayden's thighs dropped open all the way. He groaned, pushing into Shane's touch, and raked his fingernails over the tender skin at the base of Shane's spine, leaving stinging trails.

Shane gripped Kayden's cloth-covered cock and squeezed. He wanted that dick deep in his mouth, the salty sweetness of Kayden's precome on his tongue, those fingers buried in his hair, holding his head down. Shane wanted it all.

"Come with me to my room."

Kayden froze, breathing roughly. He swallowed and withdrew his hands from under Shane's shirt. "Stop. Let me up."

Shane shook his head, certain he'd misheard. "What? Kayden—"

"Let. Me. Up."

Shane growled in frustration but rolled off Kayden and sat upright, putting his head in his hands. "Fuck."

"That's all you want to do," Kayden said tightly. "Fuck." He got to his feet and swiped sand from the back of his snug black pants. "I'm not one of your goddamn groupies. Go find one of them if you just want a hole to stick your dick in."

"Kayden, that's not—"

But once again the singer stomped away and Shane didn't bother trying to finish the sentence. Kayden obviously wasn't interested in listening.

God, it made him want to scream. Shane grabbed a fistful of sand and flung it out into the water. Fuck, shit, damn, hell, and every other cussword he could think of. He'd been close. *So* close. Then he had to open his big-ass mouth and spoil everything. As usual. He should have been happy with what Kayden had given him, but instead he wanted more. *Shane the selfish asshole strikes again.* Of course the only person he screwed this time around was himself.

He sat there and stewed for a couple of minutes, then got up to go after Kayden and make sure he at least got back to the hotel safely. He hadn't exactly been clearheaded to begin with, and the anger he was obviously feeling toward Shane probably just made things worse.

Shane arrived at the hotel's front entrance in time to see Kayden board one of the elevators. He sighed and turned away. His clothes hung damp and heavy, and sand had accumulated in enough places to make walking uncomfortable. Still, he wasn't in any sort of mood to go up to his suite. He knew he wouldn't be able to sleep until he worked off his irritation. Part of it was directed at Kayden, but most of it was at himself. He shoved his hands into his pockets, bowed his head, and started down the street. In less than an hour, his night had gone from shitty to downright horrible.

Fucking *great.*

CHAPTER SEVEN

Then....
Chicago

Jesse looked up from the notebook he was writing in and glanced at the clock. Shane was late. Well, that wasn't really anything new. Shane was rarely on time for anything except their gigs. But he'd never been this late without calling before, especially not when they had plans to go out instead of just lounging around in Jesse's room, writing songs and playing music.

And kissing.

That was Jesse's favorite part. Sometimes it was all they did, just kiss and touch and whisper in the dark.

Jesse's cheeks warmed as he thought about it. God. He still couldn't believe it most days. How was it possible that Shane wanted *him*? He kept waiting to wake up from the dream, but it didn't happen.

It was true.

Shane wanted him, and he was ready and willing to

show Jesse how much any time they were together. And he told Jesse that he was sexy. Beautiful. Even though Jesse didn't really agree, he knew that whatever Shane saw in him was different than what he saw in himself. It made him feel confident. Desired. He'd never had anyone look at him the way Shane did. No matter how hard it was for him to understand sometimes, Jesse was starting to settle into the idea that what they had was for real. Maybe even forever.

They hadn't gone all the way yet. Jesse wasn't in any kind of rush. It would happen eventually. He knew that Shane wasn't a virgin and that he used to hook up with some of the guys at the bars where they played. But Shane hadn't done that since the night they first kissed.

It seemed like a millennium ago, but in reality it had only been a little over a month. Jesse wanted to. He thought about it at least five or six times a day. But he still wasn't ready to cross that line. And Shane was so respectful of that, of him. Shane never pushed. He seemed happy to let their relationship go at Jesse's pace. It was one of the many reasons Jesse loved him.

Love.

Neither one of them had said the word. It was too big, too intimidating, at least for Jesse. Shane had come close once, Jesse knew, but he hadn't been ready to hear it at the time. He stopped Shane with a kiss. But the feeling was there, unspoken between them. How could it not be? Shane was the best friend Jesse ever had. He'd been halfway in love with Shane since high school, when he realized there was so much more to Shane than the angry punk that everyone else saw.

Another glance at the clock made Jesse slam his notebook shut and push it aside. He was starting to get nervous.

What if Shane had changed his mind? They were supposed to go out for pizza and maybe catch a movie after, just the two of them. It would be the first time since they made their relationship official.

Maybe Shane wasn't ready for that kind of thing yet. It was a huge step, Jesse had to admit, going out as a couple instead of just friends. But, really, how different would it be? It wasn't as if it was a *date* really. They'd still be Shane and Jesse, hanging out like always. No one else would have to know that they were desperate to put their hands on each other.

Jesse sat up in bed and grabbed the cordless phone from his nightstand. He dialed Shane's number, feeling more and more anxious as the line kept ringing without an answer. Finally, on what must have been the fifteenth ring, someone picked up and spoke softly. "Hello?"

Jesse pressed the phone closer to his ear, gripping it in a suddenly sweaty fist. "Shane?"

"Oh, hey, Jess."

Jesse swallowed thickly. That wasn't the greeting he expected. "Is everything all right? I thought we had plans...."

There was some muffled noise on the other end of the phone, and Shane's voice got even quieter. "I can't tonight, okay? I'll see you at the gig on Sunday."

Jesse blinked. *Sunday?* But that was three days away. He hadn't gone that long without seeing Shane since back in their tutoring days. "But I—"

"I gotta go. Talk to you later."

The line went dead before Jesse could respond. Dazed, he clicked the "end" button and replaced the phone in its stand. Something was wrong. He could feel it in his gut.

Shane had pretty much hung up on him. He'd never done that before. Usually it took them half an hour to get around to saying good-bye, and most of the time they had to do the countdown thing and hang up simultaneously or they'd wind up talking until some ridiculous hour of the morning.

Jesse stood abruptly. He was out of his room and halfway down the stairs to ask his mom if he could borrow the car before he came to his senses. He hesitated at the bottom of the steps.

What are you doing? He doesn't want to see you.

What would Shane think if Jesse went rushing over there? He'd probably seem like some psycho stalker. But no. Something was up, Jesse was sure of it. They'd met for lunch the day before, between Jesse's last class and his shift at the library, and Shane had tugged him into the bathroom at the restaurant and kissed him for a few long, sweet minutes before they finally managed to pull themselves apart. You didn't just go from that to not wanting to see someone in a day. Not without a good reason. And he had to know what that reason was.

"Mom?" Jesse called into the living room. "Mind if I take your car?"

When he got to Shane's neighborhood, Jesse had to circle the block twice before he found a decent parking space. He was so distracted by his worry that he completely forgot about Shane's warning not to come to the area by himself at night—until he spotted a group of bandana-wearing Hispanic guys who were loitering on the steps of the house he was approaching and one of them got up to block his path.

Jesse slowed to a stop as the guy looked him up and down.

"You lost, *güerito?*"

Jesse just barely resisted the urge to fidget. It was hard under the weight of three different sets of eyes. "No, I'm j-just visiting a friend."

"Yeah? What friend?"

"Shane Ventura."

The guy arched an eyebrow and tilted his head, considering. "Shane, eh? Oh yeah, I've seen you around before. You're in his band."

Jesse nodded. "Yeah."

"Didn't he tell you? You should be careful coming around here after dark, kid. Some people won't be as nice as we are."

Jesse swallowed and nodded again. "He told me. But he d-doesn't know I'm coming."

The guy smirked and stepped out of his path, gesturing him forward. "Go on. We'll keep an eye on your car for you."

One of the other guys laughed and muttered something in Spanish. Jesse didn't even look his way, just kept his chin up and his shoulders straight and started walking.

It wasn't until he was knocking on Shane's door that Jesse realized how tense he'd been. He pushed his glasses up the bridge of his nose and sucked in a shuddery breath as he waited for someone to answer. A few seconds later Nick opened the door with his skateboard tucked under his arm. He looked surprised to see Jesse standing there, but not as surprised as Jesse was by the sight of him.

The right side of Nick's face was puffy and discolored, his eye swollen almost completely shut. There was a scab in the middle of his lower lip, too, and what looked to be finger-shaped bruising at the base of his throat.

Jesse was horrified. "Are y-you okay?"

Nick immediately went on the defensive. "What the fuck does it look like, genius?" He brushed past Jesse and started down the walkway. "I'm goin' to Dre's."

"Is Sh-Shane here?" Jesse called after him.

"In his bedroom," Nick answered without turning around.

Jesse stepped into the house and closed the door behind him. The interior was dark and mostly quiet, save for the faint strumming of a guitar coming from the back. He followed the sound to Shane's bedroom and knocked tentatively.

"Not now, Nicky," was the muffled response.

Jesse reached down, twisted the knob, and opened the door just wide enough to squeeze inside the room and quickly push it shut it again. He didn't think Shane's father was in the house, but he was being cautious just in case. It seemed like every time Jesse saw the man, he was pissed off about something. "It's me."

Shane was sitting on the edge of his bed with his acoustic guitar in his lap. His head jerked up at Jesse's voice and his eyes went wide.

Jesse's stomach dropped as they stared at each other in silence. Shane didn't look as bad as Nick, but he wasn't much better off. There was bruising on the right side of his face, from his temple down to the top of his cheekbone, and the area surrounding his eye was a bit puffy.

"Aww, fuck`, Jess." Shane turned his head so the bruised side was hidden. "I told you I'd see you Sunday."

Jesse crossed the room to stand in front of him. He could guess what had probably happened, but he wanted to hear it from Shane. He reached out to take the guitar from Shane's lap and rested it against the side of the nightstand.

"I was worried. Tell me what happened. Was it your dad?"

Shane was quiet for a long time. Eventually, he nodded. "Yeah. He caught Nicky with a blunt last night and he went off on him. Fuckin' asshole. Like we don't know he smokes that shit too." Shane sighed and shook his head. "Anyway, I heard what was going on and ran upstairs. I was only trying to stop him, but he thought I wanted to fight."

"I'm sorry." Jesse didn't know what else to say. He knew Shane and Nick's father hit them sometimes, but he'd never seen the evidence before now. He wondered how many times Shane might have hidden it from him in the past. "You and Nick need to get out of this house. Maybe the three of us should look into an apartment. Nick will be eighteen soon. Your dad can't keep him here after that, and there are some cheaper ones near campus. Maybe we could—"

He broke off when Shane finally turned his head to look at him again. Shane's eyes were dark with an emotion Jesse couldn't read.

"I didn't want you to see me like this," Shane said softly.

The shame in his voice hit Jesse right in the gut. He reached out to touch Shane's face, just below the bruise on his cheek. "Don't be embarrassed. This isn't your fault." Impulsively, he leaned down and brushed a soft kiss to Shane's temple. He felt Shane shudder, heard his breath catch and then rush out in a shaky exhalation.

"Jess...."

Jesse kissed him again, just the lightest touch on the corner of his mouth. "Shane, it's okay. You don't have to hide. No matter what, I—"

Shane's lips cut off the rest of his words. His arms snaked around Jesse's waist and tugged him even closer. Jesse groaned into the kiss as Shane's tongue swirled around his. He threaded his fingers into the silky hair at Shane's nape and pulled lightly.

It was different at this angle. Jesse wasn't used to being the taller one. Shane normally towered over him by a good six inches or so, but with Shane sitting on the edge of the low bed and Jesse still standing, their usual roles were reversed. It was Shane who had his head tilted back, Shane whose arms came up to loop around his neck and yank him down instead of the other way around.

They tumbled back onto the bed with Jesse falling on top of Shane. Jesse's thoughts instantly turned to how heavy he was and how Shane was probably feeling squished and uncomfortable beneath his weight. He tried to pull away, but Shane wouldn't let him. Shane's hands settled on his ass and kept him locked in place with their pelvises pressed tightly together.

Jesse might have protested if Shane's kisses weren't so very distracting. Instead he gave in to them, kissing Shane with all of the pent up lust and yearning he'd been feeling since he first realized how crazy, head-over-heels in love he was with his best friend. He'd held it inside for so long, never thinking Shane could fall for someone like him. But there they were, kissing and touching, and it was so absolutely amazing that Jesse thought his heart might just burst in his chest from the unbearable sweetness of it all.

They went on like that for long, slow minutes, the kisses getting hotter and hotter, their hands growing more and more desperate, until Shane eventually tore his mouth away and started tugging on the hem of Jesse's shirt. "Off. Want this off."

Jesse shook his head and reached down to still Shane's hands. He didn't want Shane to see his bare chest. He was pudgy. Soft. His stomach wasn't flat like Shane's, and he certainly didn't have a tight little six pack on his abs the way that Shane and Nick did.

No, I can't. It's too embarrassing.

"Shane, I don't w-want—"

Shane brushed Jesse's hands away and tugged on the shirt again. "Come on. I wanna feel you."

"B-but—"

"I thought we already talked about this, Jess."

Jesse stared down at him.

Shane's forehead wrinkled. "I mean, don't you get it? I like the way you look. I wanna see you. God, I fuckin' dream about it all the time."

"But I don't... look like you."

"No kidding." Shane rolled his eyes. "I don't want to date someone who looks like me. I want you." He reached for the bottom of Jesse's shirt again, and this time Jesse didn't stop him. "Come on, sit up."

Jesse obeyed, sitting upright on the bed. He removed his glasses and set them aside so Shane could pull the shirt over his head. When he was done, Shane stripped off his own tank top and sent it flying across the room. He didn't stop there, though. His hands went to the waistband of his jeans, and he shoved the baggy material down, leaving himself naked except for his navy blue boxers.

Jesse didn't know how he could feel so insecure and yet so turned on at the same time. Shane was perfect, all long, wiry muscle and flawless, caramel-colored skin. Even though he was almost naked, he lay there looking totally at ease. Jesse didn't blame him. If he looked like Shane, he wouldn't have any reason to be self-conscious either. As it was, though, Shane's near-nudity made him feel like every single one of his flaws was that much more pronounced.

But when he looked into Shane's eyes, he didn't see any judgment there, just heat and longing and unhidden need. Jesse felt bolder in the face of that need, so when Shane flicked a finger against the button of his cargo pants and gave him a questioning look, Jesse nodded and let Shane undo them. He lifted his hips and let Shane pull them off, and then when Shane curled his fingers into the top of Jesse's boxers and asked for permission, Jesse said that was okay too.

Seconds later Shane's boxers had joined Jesse's on the carpet and they were lying face-to-face on the bed, limbs tangled, completely naked for the first time. Jesse trembled as one of Shane's lightly furred thighs pressed between his own.

Oh God....

"This okay?" Shane whispered. His fingertips trailed up and down Jesse's spine in a slow, feathery caress.

Jesse shivered and tilted his head back so Shane could press a kiss to his throat. "Y-yeah."

Shane snuck a hand between their bodies and curled his fingers around Jesse's aching erection. Jesse shuddered at the touch, instinctively arching his back and pressing into the circle of Shane's fist.

"Tell me how far I can go, babe." Shane spoke against Jesse's ear, his lips brushing the skin with each word. He'd started up a languid stroke with his hand that made Jesse's entire body tremble. "I'm not tryin' to rush you, I swear. I just wanna make you feel good."

Jesse swallowed nervously. He wanted Shane to make him feel good. He wanted to make Shane feel good in return. There was so much he still had to learn, and he wanted Shane to be the one to teach him everything. Jesse wanted to try out all of the rest of it, he really did. But he needed things to go slow. "What do you want to do?"

Shane released Jesse's cock and slid his hand over Jesse's hip to cup one of his cheeks. He squeezed lightly, and the feel of that warm palm and those fingertips, calloused from years of playing the guitar, sent a frisson of pleasure up Jesse's back.

When one of Shane's long fingers traced his cleft and skimmed over his entrance, Jesse couldn't stop himself from burying his face against Shane's neck to hide his embarrassment. He was breathing hard and he felt like his entire body was blushing. Having Shane touch him there was both scary and exhilarating all at once.

"Do it," he whispered against the skin of Shane's throat. "Touch me."

"Yeah?" The eagerness in Shane's voice was hard to miss. "You sure?"

Jesse couldn't bring himself to look up at him. Instead he just nodded and curled one of his arms around Shane's waist.

Shane pressed a quick kiss to his temple. "Roll over, babe. Lay on your stomach."

Jesse did as Shane asked and turned his head away to face the wall. Nerves made his pulse race and blood roar in his ears. He felt the bed shift as Shane got up, heard the click of the door being locked and the sound of a drawer being opened.

The brightness from the overhead light made him feel exposed, vulnerable. When it switched off and the room was cast into darkness save for the orangey glow from one of the streetlamps outside, he almost sighed with relief. Suddenly the mood in the room seemed intimate instead of scary, and his insecurity faded a bit with the knowledge that his body was partially hidden by the shadows.

Shane settled on the mattress beside him again. Jesse sucked in a sharp breath at the feel of Shane's long, lean body pressed against his side and a big, warm hand trailing down the length of his spine.

"Tell me if you want me to stop, okay?" Shane's deep, husky voice washed over his ear.

Jesse shivered. "O-okay."

Shane's hand left his back. Jesse heard him fumbling with something, and then Shane's fingers were between his legs again, this time slick with some cool, slippery substance.

"This is just so it doesn't hurt," Shane whispered as he parted Jesse's cheeks with his fingertips and circled his entrance.

Jesse tried not to tense up. He'd never touched himself there, not for pleasure. Not even late at night when he was alone in his bedroom, thinking of Shane and stroking himself off in the dark. It felt strange, but strangely good at the same time. He wanted more.

"Do it," Jesse said, just loud enough to be heard above the whir of Shane's fan. Embarrassment heated his face despite the cover of darkness. He craved Shane's touch too much to care. Every inch of his skin felt hot and needy, every nerve ending buzzed, and his erection throbbed, trapped between his body and the mattress. He wanted to grind down, work that desperate ache against Shane's cotton sheets, but he managed to hold himself still as Shane pushed one finger inside him slowly.

"*Oh....*" Jesse trembled, burying his face in one of Shane's pillows.

"Okay? Need me to stop?"

Jesse shook his head.

Shane slid his finger in deeper. His cock was hard against Jesse's hip. "Spread your legs a bit."

Jesse shivered and did as he asked. The action let Shane slide his finger even further inside, and he touched something that made Jesse jump as if he'd been shocked.

"Oh God, wh-what—" He couldn't even finish his sentence as Shane rubbed that place again, nice and slow. Jesse couldn't stop himself from grinding down into the mattress that time. He needed... he just needed *something*. He wasn't sure what.

"Feel good?" Shane murmured.

Jesse moaned as Shane's warm breath flowed across the sweat-slick skin of his nape, raising goose bumps on his skin. "Yeah."

"I'm gonna add another finger, babe."

"'K-kay...."

Shane withdrew his finger and slowly added a second. Having two inside made it a little more uncomfortable. Jesse still didn't want Shane to stop, but he whimpered into the fabric of the pillow at the burny stretch.

"It'll get better, baby, I promise." Shane thrust subtly against Jesse's hip, mimicking the movement of his fingers as he slid them in and out. "You feel so good. So tight and hot. One day it's gonna be my cock inside you, stretching you."

Jesse shuddered at Shane's words, at the sting of a soft bite on his shoulder.

"Do you want that?" Shane said.

The only answer Jesse could give was a moan. *Yeah.* Yeah, he did want that.

"I want it." Shane nipped at one of Jesse's earlobes, just hard enough to cause a tiny bit of pain. He brushed his fingers over that wonderful, sensitive spot that made Jesse's entire body quake. "I want you so bad. I wanna feel you come with me inside." Shane slid his mouth down Jesse's throat. When he reached the base, he paused to suck lightly at the skin above Jesse's racing pulse. "Tell me you want me too."

Jesse groaned when Shane's fingers flexed. The stretching sensation had gone from discomfort to *oh God, so good*. He could hardly draw in a breath to answer, but eventually he managed a few words. "I d-do. I want you."

"You want my cock in you?" Shane moved his fingers and his hips faster, grinding hard against Jesse's side.

"Yes."

"You want me to make you come?"

Jesse trembled, pushing back into Shane's touch. "Y-yeah."

"Look at me, Jess."

Jesse forced himself to turn his head and open his eyes. Shane's face was only a couple of inches from his. The light from outside was just bright enough for Jesse to make out Shane's features—his high cheekbones, his lips, still swollen from their earlier kisses.

"You're beautiful," Shane whispered, and then he leaned forward and covered Jesse's mouth with his.

Jesse parted his lips to let Shane in. For the first time ever, Jesse didn't doubt Shane's words. He could tell by the way Shane kissed and touched him, Shane really did think he was beautiful. Shane needed him, *wanted* him. It was enough to bring tears to his eyes.

Shane broke the kiss. He panted and the rhythm of his hips grew more erratic. Jesse could tell he was close. Jesse was too, just from the feel of Shane's fingers and the friction against his cock from the mattress.

"*Jess….*" Shane groaned. "I wanna be your first and your last. No one else but me, ever."

Jesse shuddered. Shane's fingers were buried in him as deep as they could go. He was rubbing and rubbing at that spot, driving Jesse crazy.

"Promise me, Jess."

Jesse tried to talk, tried to think. His head spun. Shane was making him feel so good, so very good, it was almost impossible.

"Promise me," Shane said again.

Jesse finally choked out an answer, "I p-promise, Shane. No one else but you. Ever."

Shane groaned and shook against him. Jesse felt the warmth of Shane's release on his skin. That was all it took for him to lose it too. His back bowed and he came with his eyes squeezed shut, Shane's name tearing from his mouth on a long moan.

When the tremors stopped and Jesse's breathing calmed, Shane gently withdrew his fingers and rested his palm on the small of Jesse's back.

"Are you okay, babe? Did I hurt you?"

Jesse turned so he was facing Shane and pressed close. He nestled his head into the curve where Shane's neck met his shoulder and wrapped an arm around Shane's waist. Now that it was over, he felt suddenly shy again, but he didn't want Shane to worry. "You didn't hurt me. It felt really good."

"I didn't push too far?" Shane's voice rumbled under Jesse's cheek.

Jesse pressed even closer. "No. Not at all."

"I meant what I said. I don't ever want anyone else but you, Jess."

"I don't want anyone else either. Only you."

Shane's fingers threaded into his hair. He pulled Jesse's head back and kissed him again with slow, tender sweetness.

"I want to tell the guys," Shane whispered against Jesse's lips. It wasn't the first time he'd mentioned it. "I wanna be with you for real, Jess, out in the open. We shouldn't have to hide."

Jesse closed his eyes. He wanted that too. He was just so nervous about what Nick and Dre would think, what their parents would think. As much as he wanted it—to be out and proud and tell everyone Shane was his—he just wasn't ready to take that last step. The thought of it was too scary.

"Give me some time, okay? I just... I need a little more time."

He felt Shane's nod. "Okay. But soon, Jess. I'm tired of pretending."

"I know. I promise, Shane. Soon."

He fell asleep to the sound of Shane's heartbeat in his ear. They had the rest of their lives. Shane had said so before. They both wanted the same thing. A few more weeks couldn't cause any harm.

Soon.

Now....
Chicago

SHANE FUCKING HATED CHICAGO. Hated everything about it. Too many bad memories, too much shit with his father, too many places that he could look around the corner and swear he saw Jesse.

Jesse. Shit.

He hadn't *really* thought about Jesse in months, not

since the enigmatic Berlin had come into his life. Things had been almost great in Rome... and then in Barcelona. *Barcelona.* He'd had three very long weeks to think about that night in Barcelona. Shane had wanted to kiss Kayden so damn bad that night. Almost happened.

Shane was nervous, though. It *had* been three weeks, after all, since the almost kiss, since they kinda sorta made a connection. He'd felt it at least. He was just afraid he was going to get the same Kayden he had for most of the European tour. He really hoped not.

He was waiting for Kayden in the limo outside the Peninsula Hotel. A place he'd have been kicked out of without a second's thought if he ever tried to walk in as a kid.

They had an interview in an hour with *Rolling Stone* and were combining it with a radio appearance at the big alternative station in Chicago. Shane was far beyond caring about shit like promo interviews. He'd done so many that he could easily do them with his mind churning a mile a minute, thinking about something else. Which was good. Because he'd have to.

The car door opened, letting in a wave of Chicago summer air that made Shane want to vomit. It wasn't really the air, though. It was Kayden. His hair was all soft and spiky, his skin fresh. Shane could never get over how young he looked without all that hard stage makeup. Especially when he was smiling... *smiling.* Holy shit.

"Hey, Shane."

Shane wondered if he was hallucinating. He'd gotten a polite greeting and that smile, like Kayden was actually happy to see him.

"Hi, Kayden. Good vacation?"

"Yeah. Stopped off to see my parents. Took care of my usual stuff, you know."

"Yeah, uh, me too."

Kayden settled in, and the driver eased the car into traffic. Barcelona was hanging, heavy and somewhat awkward, between them. Shane didn't know if he should bring it up or ignore it and focus on the good fortune of Kayden seeming to finally want to be friends.

"So, have you been to Chicago before?"

Kayden let out a muffled snorting laugh and covered his mouth with his hand. "Yeah, I have."

"Why's that funny?"

"Oh, uh, I guess I've been practically everywhere by now. Just seemed like an odd question."

"Oh."

Kayden gave Shane another one of those sunshiny and disarming smiles that caught him totally off guard. What was up with him? Shane watched as he slumped back against the seat and closed his eyes, pressing gently on his eyelids.

"Jetlag is a killer," Kayden grumbled.

"Headache?"

"The worst."

"You want some ice? There's a bucket right here. We'll be there in a few minutes. Someone's bound to have an ibuprofen or two."

"Ice would be amazing, thanks—hey, why aren't we moving?"

Shane was so immersed in his own personal drama he hadn't even noticed the lack of motion. He pressed the button to lower the window and peered up at the sky.

"Aw, shit."

"What is it?" Kayden was still pressing his eyeballs. A

huge clap of thunder, followed by some honking, was the only answer Kayden needed. "Traffic jam?"

"Yeah. Shit. Looks like a big storm's about to blow in." A sudden and pounding rain on the top of the car accompanied his statement. Shane jerked back and hurriedly closed the window. "And there it is."

"Are we going to be stuck here forever?"

"No. It'll get moving. Eventually. Hey, Kayden, about Bar—"

Kayden reached up and touched Shane's lips. Shane trembled. "Can we not talk about Barcelona? I was...."

"Tipsy? I thought it was cute."

"But I—I'm just not usually like that."

Shane laughed. "So tell me more about Em and Surya."

"Did I tell you that?" Kayden looked horrified. Shane could only chuckle and nod. "I have such a big mouth."

"So, what's going on?"

"Nothing. Much to Em's irritation. At least not that they've told me."

"I thought Em was after you at first."

Kayden smiled. "No, he just needed a friend to talk to. He's totally in love with my straight drummer."

Shane cringed. "That's tough. Maybe I should talk to him about it."

"*No.* I mean, no. It's handled." Shane raised his eyebrows. "I wasn't supposed to tell you, okay?"

"What the hell?"

"It's not like that. I think Em looks up to you, Lord knows why." Kayden smiled a little. At least he was mostly joking. "He doesn't want you to see him feeling insecure."

Shane looked out the window. They hadn't gone more than about ten blocks from the hotel. "I'm really not an asshole, you know."

"I know." Kayden said it so quietly that Shane barely heard it.

IT SEEMED like an eternity before they pulled up to the radio station, probably because what should've been a ten-minute ride turned out to be nearly forty. Could've also been because the atmosphere in the limo had turned awkward and silent, like a first date that too many hopes had been pinned on. Shane thought Kayden must have been feeling it too, judging by the way he bounced out of the limo when they finally pulled up to the radio station's back entrance.

It was frustrating. They always seemed to get it almost right. Kayden was finally being nice, but the silence between them was just too charged and full of things unsaid to be comfortable.

The first thing they had to do was the radio spot, which as usual was no big deal. Shane grinned at the DJ and told slightly off-color jokes like he always did, and Kayden turned his shy British charm up to full volume. When they gave away tickets to their concert the following night while they were still on the air, there was a ton of squealing and shouting, and one poor guy accidentally hung up because he was so excited. Kayden made sure the station called him back so he could have his tickets. Of course.

After the radio show, they were ushered into the main conference room of the station and told that the reporter from *Rolling Stone* was caught in the same traffic jam they were in. He was allegedly only a few blocks away and would be there as soon as possible.

"Might as well just get out and walk at this point," Shane grumbled. He was hungry, and he didn't much feel like waiting. On the other hand, he *did* have Kayden all to himself, which was rare.

Kayden shot him a small smile. "Hey, it's not so bad. At least the building has air-conditioning. It gets so hot and humid during these storms."

"You've been in one before?"

Kayden simply nodded and pulled out his phone. He sat quietly for a few minutes, staring intently at the screen.

"Whatcha doin'?" Shane couldn't stand the silence.

"Reading."

"On your phone?"

Kayden cracked another smile. "You can read on your phone too. I'm guessing you haven't tried, though."

"Nah. Maybe I'm old, but I like paper books still."

"You read? I was assuming you—"

Shane held up his hand. "You don't really know me, Kayden. Do me the favor of not jumping to conclusions." Shane had no idea why he pulled out those words from a million years ago, but they felt right.

Kayden's eyes widened. "I guess you're right. I'm—"

The lights flickered, and Shane could hear a muffled boom from outside. He wished the conference room had windows. He'd always liked watching the storms when he was a kid.

Kayden shuddered and drew his arms around his knees. He had his feet propped up on the chair in front of him. In that pose, he looked so young, almost like the little boy Shane imagined he'd once been.

"Don't like storms?" Shane asked. He'd suspected as much that night in Rome.

"Not my favorite."

With that, there was another clap of thunder, and the lights died. It was pitch black in the room. Even better, the comforting whir of the air conditioner went completely silent.

"Sh-Shane?"

"I'm here. You want to try to go out in the hall? Find someone else?"

"Yeah. We should. But I'm fine. Here." A bright light came from Kayden's phone. "Flashlight app."

Shane could see Kayden's grin in the glow that lit him from below. Shane took the phone and peeked out into the hallway. It too was black and still, the only noise a soft scurrying that came from the direction of the sound booth.

"There's no one out there." Shane pulled the door shut and handed the phone back to Kayden.

"Yeah, you think? This place is dead. Let's just stay here. The lights will come on in a minute."

Shane nodded and backed up to the wall. He sank into a seated position and was surprised when Kayden slid down and settled on the floor right next to him.

"The great Kayden Berlin afraid of thunderstorms?"

He got nothing in return but a less-than-gentle pinch. Then Kayden's warm and slightly damp arm bumped against his. *He moved closer.* Shane loved that Kayden's impulse when he was upset was to get closer rather than farther away.

"Hey." Shane reached up in the dark and swept a thumb across Kayden's cheek. "It's no big deal."

"I know."

"Then why'd you come over here?"

Kayden exhaled slowly. "Because I wanted to."

And then, before Shane had a chance to react, Kayden's warm hand cupped his jaw, and a thumb traced the curve of his lower lip. Shane's nerves sang arias.

"Kay—"

Shane was cut off by lips, soft and faintly orange-flavored, brushing against his, and a tentative tongue slipping out to taste.

"Wish I didn't want this," Kayden whispered against Shane's mouth.

"But you do." Shane couldn't stand the anticipation any longer. He reached up and tugged on Kayden's neck, pulling him closer until his nose was nestled right in the place next to Shane's and they were breathing the same breath.

And that was when, there in the still darkness, it happened. Everything Shane had been wanting, needing, since that very first day in London. His lips were on Kayden's; his tongue was sneaking tastes. He took Kayden's arms and looped them around his own neck and shivered at how amazing it felt.

"This is just like I r—"

"Hmm?" Shane was barely listening, too wrapped up in how amazing he felt.

"I thought it would be like this," Kayden whispered, then nipped softly at Shane's lower lip. Shane didn't have to be asked twice. He opened his mouth to deepen the kiss. It was perfect, maybe even more than he imagined it would be. Like coming home. Shane kept waiting for Kayden to pull away, to jump up and scramble backward. It didn't happen. He just kept kissing, tasting, threading his fingers into Shane's hair.

They were still kissing long minutes later when the fluorescent lights popped on with a dull crackle. Kayden pulled away, and Shane had to give him credit. He didn't jump up; he didn't look horrified—just a bit scared, wide-eyed, and surprised. Shane reached up to cup his cheek. Kayden trembled and backed away.

"Um, we should go see if the *Rolling Stone* guy made it," he mumbled, smoothing his hair and wiping at his mouth with the back of his hand.

"Yeah, let's go see."

THE CHICAGO NIGHT WAS OPPRESSIVE—HOT, dark, and heavy—and filled with steam from the earlier storm and pollution from the many cars that clogged the streets below. But there was a pleasant breeze on the terrace at the hotel, where they were having the kickoff party for the Lucky Moon Tour's North American leg. It was almost as if the privileged few who were allowed on the terrace were better than the rest of the city, better than those regular folk who had to swelter through the summer heat wave down below.

The tour management thought it was fitting to have the first show in Luck's hometown. Shane didn't give a shit. He just wanted to get the Chicago show over with and move on.

Shane was looking forward to seeing Kayden again. He still didn't know how to process what happened that morning. Kayden hadn't really said much about it on the way back to the hotel. Then Shane's phone rang, and they arrived, and everything he wanted to say seemed to float away on the humid breeze.

At least he had another chance. He scanned the rooftop club, searching for a shock of white-blond hair in the crowd. He only saw a sea of people, punctuated by glowing gold fabric lanterns and billowing red curtains that flowed around low, cushioned benches, giving the whole place the illusion of romance and privacy.

Shane was sitting on a bench near the bar, attempting to hide from the crowd. He didn't want to play the customary social butterfly role, although the point of the party was to see and be seen. He didn't want to see anybody other than Kayden. A groupie who looked vaguely familiar kept hovering, trying to get his attention. He wanted to swat the guy away like an annoying fly.

"Mr. Ventura, would you like another drink?" Speaking of annoying flies....

"No, thanks—"

"Reggie."

"No thanks, Reggie."

"I could always make you one upstairs." Reggie the groupie gave Shane a hopeful look.

"Maybe another time," he answered absentmindedly. Shane had just seen a glowing blond head come onto the terrace through the tall glass double doors that were guarded on both sides by heavy security. Kayden. He wanted to rush over—run, actually—if it wouldn't make him look like a total fool.

For the moment, he stayed where he was, watching Kayden and the other members of Moonlight work the crowd. He knew he would have a hard time getting to them —the lucky fans in attendance were swarming, and the record label people were doing the usual handshake, kiss-ass routine—but he couldn't stop himself from staring and willing all of those damn sycophants away so he could get closer.

He was jarred from his thoughts by a painful elbow in his side. *Fuck. Nicky.*

"What the hell, dude? You're all, like, wet for him and shit."

Shane groaned quietly. Not the conversation he wanted to be having. "Hey. You like the party? I saw you doing shots with Dre earlier."

"Good try, bro. What up with you and Popsicle Pants?

Has it completely slipped your mind that he's a total asshole? Hot, yeah, but an ice queen."

"I don't know what's up. We were starting to get to know each other in Europe. It was nice. Then the break, and now? I'm not sure." There was no way in hell he was telling his brother about that morning.

"Is he a good fuck at least?"

Shane gave Nick a smack on the side of his head. "Is that all you think about?"

"Well *yeah*. Isn't that all any guy thinks about? Please tell me you're at least fucking him."

"No, not yet. And some of us might actually have feelings for people."

Nick snorted. "Some of us are g-a-y."

"Fuck off. Go find a chick to blow you or something."

"Seriously, what's up with you?"

Shane sighed and watched Kayden's blond head bob through the crowd, surrounded by his black-clad entourage. "I don't know."

"You *do* want to fuck him, right?"

"God, do you have to call it that? But, yeah, of course I do. I *am* human. It's more, though. I want to talk to him and get to know him, play music with him, you know...."

"Could you have a bigger vag? Listen, drool over him as much as you want. I just don't want the tour to be ruined if you fag out on me and get all emo. Be cool, okay? I don't wanna have to join another band."

Shane rolled his eyes. He was so used to Nicky's mouth by now that it was hard to be offended. "I'll be cool. Try to keep the vag put away and shit. Oh, and Nicky?"

Nick looked up.

"If you call me emo again, I'll kick your ass... or there's always the potential for a good nut-sac waxing."

"In your dreams, pretty boy." Nick chuckled and punched him in the arm. "Have fun with your girlfriend."

Shane gave his brother a silent middle finger and slid off his bar stool to go in search of Kayden.

THE COOL, down-the-nose stare he received when he approached Kayden was nothing like what Shane expected. He'd hoped, especially after earlier, that their fragile friendship was finally going somewhere, and maybe, despite Kayden's protests, it would turn into more. A lot more.

"Uh, hi, Kayden." Shane was desperately hoping he was wrong about the look he just received.

"Ventura."

Shit. He wasn't.

"How was the rest of your day?"

Kayden just gave Shane a look that said *Why are you talking to me like we're friends?*

"It was tolerable. I trust yours was the same. Now, if you'll excuse me."

Kayden walked away without another word, leaving Shane feeling like his gut had been ripped out. *What happened to this morning?*

He stumbled back toward the bar with only one thought in his head—he needed tequila, enough to drown in. Enough to dull the raw ache in his stomach. The idea of drinking himself into oblivion was the only thing that could penetrate the shocked fog in his brain.

"Mr. Ventura? Shane?"

Shane looked up when he heard his name. That same little groupie from before, Roger or something, was sitting at a low table a few yards from the bar. He grinned at Shane.

"Oh. Hey, Roger."

"Reggie, but that's okay. You can call me whatever you want. Do you want to sit down?" Reggie patted the seat next to him.

Shane was about to say no but paused when he felt the weight of someone's gaze on his back. He glanced over his shoulder and saw Kayden staring at him through a gap in the crowd. The knowledge that Kayden was watching made him change his mind. Shane sank down onto the low, cushioned bench next to his fan and leaned close to whisper in the kid's ear, making sure to visibly drag his thumb down a pale, freckly neck. "Will you go get me a shot? Tequila. The best they've got."

"Sure."

Roger or Reggie or whatever the hell his name was bounced up and trotted off toward the bar. Shane smiled and silently saluted Kayden. It didn't take but a minute for his drink to be returned. He waved the lime away and took the shot straight, no frills. It burned pleasantly.

Shane saw that his hopeful and persistent fan had the lime between his teeth. *What the hell? Why not?* He leaned forward and sucked on the lime before removing it and giving his eager partner a long, lusty kiss. He kept his eyes open the whole time, watching Kayden for a reaction. He expected jealousy, or anger, *something*, when he slid his hand under what's-his-name's shirt and caressed a smooth back.

What Shane didn't expect was the look of pure disgust and sharp turn followed by Kayden exiting the party at a near-run pace.

Shit! That wasn't the reaction Shane had been hoping for. He tossed Roger-Robert-Reggie aside and jumped up. He pushed and wove his way through the crowd, trying to get to the doors into the main hotel area. It was frustrating;

he felt like every other person wanted him to stop and talk. Shane just waved them away and kept going, desperate to get to the doors and to Kayden. When he finally did, he saw Kayden all the way on the other side of the lobby area, standing alone near the bank of elevators. He started sprinting across the rich red-and-gold-patterned carpet.

"Kayden!" Shane shouted, tripping over a plush leather ottoman and not caring if he looked ridiculous running across the lobby of a very expensive hotel. "Wait!"

Kayden didn't even turn.

Shane caught up just as Kayden was stepping into the elevator. He slipped inside before Kayden had the chance to hit the Door Close button.

"What do you want?" Kayden sounded like he was gritting his teeth.

"I want to know what happened out there."

Kayden stayed silent, and Shane watched the numbers on the floor counter slip by. The elevator doors slid open when the counter read PH, and Kayden stalked into the hallway without a word.

"What happened, Kayden? You have to at least tell me." Shane ran after him, not wanting to be stuck outside in the hall with no answers.

"I don't know. Looks to me like you had your tongue down some guy's throat. I would've at least hoped you could keep your dick in your pants for ten whole minutes."

"What? Was that a fucking *test* or something? I didn't want him. I want you! I've wanted you for months, but you treated me like this morning never happened, and then—" Shane dropped off, at a loss for how to explain what he was feeling. He hated how lost he sounded. *Shit.*

"Well, if it was a test, you failed spectacularly. Were you trying to make me jealous?"

"Did it work?"

Kayden growled, literally growled, then fisted his hand in Shane's shirt. "God, you're a pain in the ass. C'mere."

With that, he pulled Shane into his sumptuous penthouse suite and kicked the door shut behind him.

CHAPTER EIGHT

"You're such a child." Kayden shoved at Shane's shoulders. "Where do you get off, trying to play games with me?"

Shane stumbled back a couple of steps and reached out to steady himself on a nearby table. Anger rose as Kayden stared at him, that all too familiar expression of disdain on his face.

"Dammit, there wouldn't be any need for games if you would just admit how you feel."

"Admit to how I feel?" Kayden scoffed. "There's nothing to admit to."

"That's a fucking lie, and you know it." Shane breathed roughly, his hands fisted at his sides. "That night in Rome, and that day in Barcelona, you were so... *different*. Then this morning you kissed me, you told me you wanted me. That's why you acted the way you did out there just now, isn't it? You want me as much as I want you. And that fucking *terrifies* you."

"You presume way too much." Kayden's tone was frigid. "Yes, my body responds to yours. I won't deny it. I can't. But that kiss was a mistake. It should never have happened, and it will *never* happen again. I told you once before—and you just reminded me why with your little act downstairs—I want *nothing* to do with you."

"Oh yeah?" Shane advanced on Kayden, his movements predatory. Kayden's eyes widened, and he took a step back, but trapped between Shane and the door, there was nowhere left for him to run. Shane didn't stop until their chests were touching and Kayden was forced to tilt his head back to look up at him. "Fucking prove it, then."

He slammed his mouth onto Kayden's and kissed him hard. Kayden's lips were parted, and Shane took advantage of that fact and slipped his tongue inside. He kissed Kayden with all the pent-up frustration that seethed in his body, with every last drop of desire and yearning, with all the desperation he felt during their long months touring overseas.

At first Kayden went rigid against him, making a muffled sound of protest. Shane just pressed closer and kept kissing him. It was rough, angry, nothing like the slow, tender kisses from earlier that morning, but he felt Kayden start to respond—his body softening, his lips parting further to allow Shane more access—and then Kayden suddenly seemed to remember himself and pushed him away.

"No." Kayden panted, holding out a hand to ward Shane off. "I'm not going to do this with you."

Shane groaned and raked his fingers through his hair. "Why? What the fuck is so wrong with me?"

"I already *told* you," Kayden said tightly, his accent thicker than Shane had ever heard it. "You are such a bloody cliché, a typical rock star with the usual vices—sex, drugs, alcohol. You don't even have it in you to be original. I've read the tabloids. I've seen the pictures. You might as well install a revolving door in your bedroom to accommodate all of the different groupies you have coming and going. Why should I want to be involved with someone like you?"

Shane flinched at the words. Rage and hurt warred for dominance inside him. Eventually his anger won out. "You think that's all I am? Some stereotypical rocker, all gloss and no substance? What makes you any better? You gonna stand there and tell me that you don't have any faults? That you're never weak? You've never made a goddamn mistake?"

"No. I'm not perfect." Kayden stepped closer and jabbed Shane in the chest with a finger. "But I don't spend all my free time getting pissed. I don't have a different man in my bed every night. I don't fuck for sport."

Kayden's cheeks were flushed, his mouth swollen, his eyes fierce. Shane didn't know what possessed him to reach out and grab Kayden's shoulders—maybe it was aggravation; maybe it was just the lust that'd been driving him crazy for so long—but he jerked the other singer to him and claimed his mouth again. Despite all his talk, Kayden reacted almost immediately, kissing Shane back. He gripped Shane's shirt in clenched fists, and it took him a lot longer to pull away than the first time, as if for just a few seconds, he forgot why he was fighting so hard.

When he finally managed to tear his mouth from Shane's, Kayden looked furious with himself. "I can't do this. I want you to go."

"No. Not until you listen to what I have to say."

Kayden glared at Shane, his expression frosty. "I don't want to hear it. I don't care."

"You do care. Otherwise you wouldn't be so pissed."

Kayden made a scornful noise and opened his mouth to speak, but Shane cut him off.

"Don't deny it. You're mad because you hate the thought of me being with someone else. Why can't you see? If you paid me even the slightest bit of attention, I would never even *look* at anyone else again."

Kayden shook his head. "Stop." He stepped up to Shane and curled a hand around his nape, then drew Shane's head down. "Just shut up."

Before Shane could respond, Kayden's mouth was on his. There was fury in that kiss, yes, but hunger too, raw and sensual. Kayden bit Shane's lower lip, sucked on his tongue. He dropped his free hand to cup Shane's cock through his pants and stroked the thick length into painful hardness.

Shane pushed into Kayden's palm and a noise that sounded suspiciously like a whimper escaped his throat. He'd wanted Kayden's hands on him for so long, it'd become a physical ache, a yearning so deep, he could feel it in his marrow. It made him frantic, desperate for more contact, more kisses, more *everything*.

Pain prickled along Shane's scalp as Kayden's fingers tightened in his hair to hold him in place as they kissed. Kayden devoured Shane's mouth, mastering him, owning him so thoroughly Shane could only moan helplessly and try to press closer. His hips jerked as Kayden continued to stroke him through his fly. But it wasn't enough. Shane wanted bare skin, warm and smooth under his palms. He reached down to grab the hem of Kayden's black shirt and tug it upward. They broke apart so Shane could pull the shirt over Kayden's head and toss it aside.

Shane went for another kiss, but Kayden shook his head. He turned his attention to undoing Shane's pants instead. Then he shoved the material down and leaned up to tongue the hollow at the base of Shane's throat.

"You're so fucking irritating," he said against the tender

skin there, but he slipped a hand into Shane's boxers, curving his fingers around Shane's erection to take the sting from the words. "No one has ever pissed me off more than you."

Shane groaned, tipping his head back as Kayden pressed kisses along his neck. "I wouldn't, uh, affect you so strongly if you didn't—*oh hell yeah*—if you didn't feel something for me."

Kayden laughed dryly, roughly jerking Shane's cock in his fist. "Yeah, I feel something. Annoyance."

"Liar." Shane captured Kayden's mouth again and kissed him, wild and reckless. He gripped the waistband of Kayden's tight low-rise pants and pushed them down, not even bothering with buttons or zippers. The fabric fell and pooled around Kayden's ankles. He was naked underneath, and the very idea of Kayden going commando made Shane's dick throb.

Shane stepped back, away from Kayden's touch, so he could take in the view of that long, lean body. Kayden's skin was pale white underlain by the slightest hint of peach, every inch of him hairless and silky smooth. His cock was perfect, deep pink, well proportioned, extending arrow-straight from his groin. Shane wanted it in his mouth, wanted to fall to his knees and worship it.

"You... you're so...."

Words failed. So Shane gave in to the demands screaming through his body. He fell to his knees, his movements less than graceful, pants hanging half-open, and dropped a soft kiss on head of that flawless cock. Kayden shivered, and it was all the encouragement Shane needed to take the damp tip of Kayden's cock into his mouth. Precome leaked onto his tongue, and Shane moaned at the sweet, salty taste.

Kayden made a low, breathy sound. His hips jerked as Shane alternated between long, slow sucks and delicate flicks of his tongue across the glans. Shane worked his mouth over Kayden's length, took him as far as he could go, and hummed around that velvety skin.

He felt a moment of regret for the fact that he'd never mastered the art of deep throating. If he could do that—take Kayden all the way, feel Kayden pull his hair and fuck his mouth like a porn star until Kayden came warm and slick down the back of his throat—it would be beyond hot. Shane nearly came himself just thinking about it, sucking hard until Kayden's fingers dug painfully into the muscles of his shoulders.

"Stop. I'm too close...."

Shane drew back slowly, releasing the tip with a *pop* and a final swirl of his tongue around the ridge.

Kayden shuddered and reached down to grab Shane's arms and urge him to his feet. Once Shane was standing, Kayden stripped off his shirt and trailed wet, openmouthed kisses across Shane's lightly defined pecs. Shane cupped Kayden's tight little ass and yanked him close. He was still half-dressed, and Kayden's pants were tangled around his ankles, but they managed to stumble across the suite to one of the plush leather couches in the sitting area. They fell onto it in a heap of limbs, grinding, undulating against each other, their movements frenzied.

"I have to be inside you," Shane whispered between kisses. "I have to feel you around me."

Kayden stiffened in his arms. He pulled back and met Shane's gaze, his green eyes dark with an emotion Shane couldn't decipher. "No. Tonight, you don't fuck me. I fuck *you*."

Shane stared up at Kayden, his mouth suddenly bone

dry. In his thirty-one years, he'd never allowed anyone to top him, and before Kayden, he never actually wanted to. Kayden was the only man he'd ever imagined above him, holding him down, in his body. Shane licked his lips, an instinctive, nervous gesture. "Okay."

Kayden slid off him and bent down to remove his shoes and kick his pants away from his ankles. Shane sat upright and unlaced his boots, tugged them off, and dropped his socks into them before setting them aside.

"Come on." Kayden held out a hand, and Shane accepted it, allowing Kayden to pull him up and lead him into the bedroom.

Once there, Kayden kissed him again, backing Shane up until they were next to the bed. He shoved Shane's shoulders, breaking the kiss, and Shane fell back onto the mattress with a bounce. Kayden followed him down, scattering kisses across Shane's toned abdomen. He paused to rub his cheek on the light happy trail that started under Shane's navel.

"I've imagined this so many times," he murmured. "I love the way you smell, the way you feel." His voice was so soft, Shane thought he'd misheard. But then Kayden looked up at him, and his eyes smoldered.

Shane felt the heat of that gaze slide over him like a caress. He quivered, his body nearly vibrating with lust and anticipation, as he watched Kayden move lower.

Kayden parted the flaps of his pants and mouthed Shane's cock through the thin cotton of his boxers. When Kayden blew over the damp material, Shane groaned and his eyelids fluttered shut. He felt Kayden's fingers curl into the waistband of his boxers; then Kayden tugged them off, taking Shane's pants along with them.

The air-conditioning in the bedroom was cranked high,

the temperature icy cool. Shane trembled as it washed over his skin, at the contrast of Kayden's warm palms running up the insides of his legs, parting his thighs. But then the touch was abruptly removed, and all that was left was the cold.

"J.A.S.," Kayden said in an odd voice.

"Huh?" Shane blinked in confusion, registering only the fact that Kayden had stopped touching him and that his skin already mourned the loss. He looked down to see that Kayden's green eyes were focused on his right hip. Shane's mind was clouded by lust and moving slowly. It took him a few seconds to realize what must have caught Kayden's attention and process what he said. "Oh."

Kayden was staring at his tattoo, the one that all of the members of Luck had gotten to celebrate the release of their first album. It was a tribal four-leaf clover done in black and green. They all had the tattoos done at the same time, but in a moment of pure sentimentality, Shane had Jesse's initials added at the base of his clover. At the time, he hadn't been sure if it was for repentance or remembrance, but he'd never regretted it. He'd known then that, in spite of what happened, Jesse would always own a part of his heart. Maybe even his soul too.

Shane realized Kayden's eyes had moved to his face, and he appeared to be waiting for some kind of answer. "Uh... those are my best friend's initials."

"Your best friend," Kayden repeated flatly.

"Yeah, uh, well, he *was* my friend. A long time ago."

Kayden didn't say anything else, just leaned down to trace the lines of the tattoo with his tongue. The soft skin of his cheek brushed against Shane's rigid cock. Shane bit his lip, letting his head fall back as Kayden lingered over the tattoo, scraping his teeth over the inked skin. Kayden palmed his erection, and Shane shuddered, his hips jolting when Kayden turned his head and finally, *finally*, put that hot, wet mouth right where he needed it most.

Kayden licked the underside of his shaft from base to tip, then took Shane's entire length in one smooth motion. Shane made an incoherent sound, barely resisting the urge to slam up into the tight, slick heat of Kayden's throat and just take what he wanted. But when Kayden swallowed around his cockhead, Shane couldn't stop himself from burying his fingers in Kayden's white-blond hair and tugging roughly at the silky strands, silently demanding more.

Shane would have never expected something like this from the cold, aloof Kayden he'd known for most of the tour. But from the brief glimpses he'd gotten of the *real* Kayden, during those rare, unguarded moments when Kayden's mask slipped away, maybe it shouldn't have been a surprise. He should have been able to guess there'd be fire burning beneath Kayden's icy exterior. He hoped Kayden would let it go, give in to it, and let the resultant blaze consume them both.

Kayden sucked him hard and fast, pressing one hand down on Shane's pelvis while slipping the fingers of the other under Shane's balls to stroke the delicate skin there. Shane sensed his orgasm rising, his sac drawing up tight, shivery warmth pooling low in his groin. Just when he started to crest, Kayden pulled off his cock and wrapped his fingers around the base, squeezing tightly enough to hurt.

Shane cried out, bowing his back off the mattress. Kayden had managed to prevent his orgasm—barely—but Shane was still desperate to come, his dick hypersensitive and throbbing. He panted in frustration, craving the slick glide of Kayden's mouth on him again.

Kayden gave him just enough time to recover, holding

those intense green eyes steady on Shane's face, before he placed his hands on Shane's thighs and pushed his legs apart. As Shane watched and wondered what he planned, Kayden dipped his head and briefly nuzzled his balls. Then he moved down, lower, and laved at Shane's entrance with slow, drenched licks until the muscle relaxed enough for him to press his tongue inside.

Shane groaned long and low, writhing on the sheets as Kayden worked him with that clever tongue. "Oh God." The sight of Kayden's pale blond head between his thighs was almost too much. Shane took his cock in hand and gave it a rough yank. "Oh fuck."

Kayden tormented him with lips, teeth, and tongue for a few more moments. When he pulled back, put a finger in his mouth, and sucked briefly, Shane didn't even have time to get nervous before Kayden slipped it inside him, pushing firmly past that tight ring of muscle. Shane shivered at the sensation and let his eyelids fall shut. He'd been fingered before, but it'd been a *very* long time, and it never went any further than that. He never trusted anyone enough to allow it. But he wanted Kayden so badly, more than he could ever remember wanting anyone or anything, enough to let him be the first. And hopefully he'd be the last. The only.

"Relax," Kayden said softly. "You've never bottomed before, have you?"

"No." Oddly, Shane felt his cheeks warm in a blush. He would have thought he'd be beyond blushing after all the crazy shit he'd done in his life, both in bed and out, but Kayden made him feel vulnerable, exposed in a way no one ever had. Not since Jesse.

"I'll take care of you. Be right back."

Shane nodded but kept his eyes shut. He felt Kayden withdraw his finger and sensed him moving around the room. A few seconds later, the mattress dipped, and the heat of Kayden's body was flush against his side. Kayden skimmed a hand over his hip, the only warning Shane had before Kayden's fingers were at his hole again, this time slick with something cool and slippery. He pressed in with two, and the searing stretch was enough to make Shane stiffen instinctively.

"Relax," Kayden whispered against his cheek.

Shane turned his head and blindly sought out Kayden's mouth. The feel of Kayden's tongue sliding over his was enough to distract him from the discomfort.

Kayden kissed him deeply, and without the underlying anger from before, the feel of it was hot and sweet and *so fucking right* it made Shane's chest ache. He'd only ever experienced one other kiss that matched it: that very first one with Jesse, the one that woke him up and changed everything.

Shane lost himself in that kiss, the feel of Kayden's fingers inside him, the hardness of Kayden's cock against his side. He cupped Kayden's nape in one hand, keeping their mouths locked together, and kissed Kayden until they were both breathless. Only when his mouth felt bruised and tender did he allow Kayden to pull away. He opened his eyes to watch as Kayden trailed kisses down his chest. Kayden paused at the tattoo again, nipped at the skin, and then soothed the hurt with his tongue. While he was doing that, Shane saw him reach for one of the foil packets lying on the bed beside his leg.

Shane watched through half-closed eyes as Kayden knelt upright, tore open the packet, and slid the condom on. He grabbed the tube of lubricant from where it rested on the mattress and squeezed a generous portion into his palm before slicking it over the latex. He kept his gaze on Shane's face the entire time. Without speaking, he urged Shane to roll onto his side and draw his knees toward his chest. Shane closed his eyes again and let Kayden maneuver him. Kayden's fingers brushed over him once more, spreading slickness, and then the blunt tip of his cock was there. Shane sucked in a breath as Kayden began to push in slowly.

Despite the work of Kayden's tongue and fingers, it stung. Shane moaned at the feel of being stretched so full, unable to decide if he liked it or hated it. Then a hand trailed soothingly down his back, and he remembered this was Kayden inside him. Kayden, who he'd wanted for what felt like forever. Kayden, who he'd dreamed of taking and being taken by.

"Okay?" Kayden asked once he was all the way inside.

Shane nodded. "Yeah."

Kayden gripped his hip and started to move, first withdrawing nearly all the way, then sliding back in. The tempo increased, and soon the sting faded a bit, transformed into a feeling that was more pleasure than discomfort. When the head of Kayden's cock hit his prostate, it sent a shock of electricity through his system.

Shane's body spasmed; his limbs trembled. Kayden was pressed as deep as he could go, grinding in tight little circles, brushing that spot again and again. It felt good, beyond his imagining, but it was almost too much, an intensity that flirted too closely with pain. And then Kayden grabbed one of his knees and lifted his leg, altering the position, and suddenly Shane couldn't get enough. He shoved down, meeting Kayden's shallow thrusts. His skin felt hot, stretched tight over his muscles. Every part of him that touched Kayden burned, and the only thing he could think was he needed *more*.

Shane reached down and wrapped his fingers around his own shaft. He stroked slowly, savoring the sensation as he used his thumb to spread the drops of liquid that had beaded at the tip.

"*Kayden*. Fuck me."

Kayden's movements picked up speed, and he leaned over Shane's body, grabbed a handful of Shane's hair, and tugged his head back. He pressed his open mouth to Shane's throat and sucked at the tender skin. The sound of their harsh breathing filled the room. Normally Shane wasn't very vocal during sex, but something about Kayden brought it out of him. He moaned like he was dying, squeezing his eyes shut tight as Kayden's thrusts brought their bodies together over and over again.

"*Fuck*. Oh yeah... good. So good."

Kayden's only response was to move faster. He slid his lips down to the curve where Shane's neck met his shoulder and bit him there, deep, and hard enough that Shane's mouth fell open in a gasp. The shock of it pushed Shane over the edge into his orgasm. His body went rigid, his cock pulsed in his hand, and he came everywhere—all over his fingers, his chest, the sheets.

Kayden's rhythm faltered for a second, and he groaned as Shane's inner muscles clamped around him. He yanked Shane's head back farther, kissing him fiercely, and it was heat and honey and sex. Helpless against the onslaught of emotions that flooded into his body, all Shane could do was kiss him back. He had a brief instant of clarity, one second during that whirlwind kiss when realization came to him swift and certain. Somehow, somewhere along the way, though he couldn't pinpoint when, or even explain it, he'd started falling for Kayden Berlin.

The knowledge was there and gone in a flash because

Kayden was still inside him, still moving fast. And Shane wanted it to go on, to keep Kayden inside him forever. But a few thrusts later, Kayden tore his mouth away and buried his face against Shane's throat, fine tremors running through his body as he came.

Once Kayden's shivers abated, he withdrew and shifted so he lay beside Shane. Even as gentle as Kayden was, Shane couldn't prevent his wince. He was sore enough to know he'd still be feeling it come morning, maybe even for a day or two. But that was just fine. It was a delicious kind of soreness, and he welcomed it, embraced it. Because that moment, when Kayden had pounded into him and kissed Shane as if he'd never, ever stop, was one of the hottest of Shane's life. Hell, who was he kidding? It had been *the* hottest, without question.

They rested there for a few minutes, breathing roughly as their bodies cooled. Shane took comfort in the warm press of Kayden's chest against his back, but Kayden eventually pulled away and got up without a word. He crossed the suite to go into the bathroom and returned a short while later with a damp towel. He used it to clean Shane off, his touch surprisingly gentle. When he finished, he tossed it onto the floor and got back into bed. Shane wanted to turn to him, to draw Kayden into his arms and hold him tight, but he hesitated. Most men he'd been with weren't snuggly after sex, and Shane would ordinarily include himself in that number, but he wanted that intimacy now, wanted to fall asleep skin to skin. Kayden took the decision out of his hands when he reached over to the bedside table and switched off the light, then closed the gap between them and curled an arm around Shane's waist. Shane shifted so they were facing each other and slid his fingers into the downy hair at Kayden's nape.

"Kayden—"

"Shh. Don't. Just sleep."

Shane felt a brief pang of hurt, even though he'd started speaking without really knowing what he wanted to say. He pushed the feeling away, inwardly berating himself. What? Not only did he want to cuddle after sex, but now he wanted to talk too? Shane grinned self-deprecatingly, glad the action was hidden in the darkness.

He had it bad.

Surprisingly, the awareness didn't bring with it the panic he'd felt when he first realized he wanted more from Kayden than just a casual fuck. Yeah, he had it bad, all right. And he didn't even mind. All that remained was to convince Kayden that they belonged together. But Shane thought maybe, just maybe, Kayden already knew.

CHAPTER NINE

Then....
Chicago

"How could you, Shane?"

Jesse's gut was being ripped in two. Literally. There couldn't be any other explanation for why he felt like he was dying. Shane was kicking him out of the band, *their* band, the one they built together. That band was Jesse's whole life. No, fuck that. *Shane* was Jesse's whole life, and he'd just told Jesse he and the band were moving to New York to start recording and get into the music scene. He didn't say a damn thing about taking Jesse with him.

"I couldn't do anything about it. They made it a condition of our contract." Shane's voice sounded cold, impersonal.

It was wrong, all wrong. Jesse wanted to believe he didn't mean it. He wanted to believe the whole thing was just a dumb, cruel joke and any second Shane would laugh and say "just kidding baby, we're all leaving together," but he didn't. Nothing. No smile, no hug, not a fucking joke.

"You could have fought for me. You could have told them to fuck off and you'd find another label." Jesse would've done anything for Shane.

"That shit gets around. We would've been blackballed, dead before we even had a chance to start. You know that."

"I know that you're picking a fucking business deal over me." It was more than that. To be honest, part of Jesse had been waiting for this moment since the first time he and Shane kissed. He didn't know why he was surprised.

Shane shrugged. "It is what it is. I don't have any choice."

"No. It doesn't have to be this way. You *do* have a choice."

"There is no other way. You have other options. Nicky and I don't. I can't pass on the chance to get him away from my dad. How long will it be before Nicky goes too far and my dad completely loses his shit? I've gotta get him out." Shane paused, and Jesse saw his throat work, the hard bob of his Adam's apple. For a moment he felt a quick flare of hope. Then Shane went on in that same casual tone. "Besides, it's just a band. I barely got through high school. You can finish college. Make something of yourself."

"It's not just the band, Shane. What have these past few months been to you? What did I mean to you? What were we?"

Shane didn't answer. Jesse was losing the fight for control, struggling to keep from falling on the ground or burying himself in Shane's arms and begging him to reconsider. But he couldn't. He had some pride, and apparently Shane had a responsibility to his brother that meant more than anything he and Jesse had shared. Blood came first.

"Shane... please don't do this. Are you trying to rip me in half? 'Cause that's what you're doing."

Jesse saw a tiny crack in Shane's expression, but just like that it disappeared, and Shane's old I don't give a shit look was right back on his face.

"Look, we signed the contract last night. It's over, Jesse." Not Jess, not Jay, but Jesse. Shane hadn't called him that in years, not since they were practically strangers. It felt awful.

Jesse couldn't do anything but stare.

Now….
Chicago

*"W*HAT DID *I mean to you, Shane? What were we? What did I mean to you?"*

Love. Happiness. Everything in the world.

Shane turned to once again walk away from the best friend he ever had. It wasn't any easier than the first time or any of the others. He'd been reliving that moment over and over for years. He had to keep walking before he broke down and begged Jesse to forgive him. He wanted to turn around. He wanted to turn around…

Yes. Do it. Turn around, you fool. Leaving Jesse was the biggest mistake you ever made.

"Why'd you do it, Shane? Why did you leave me?"

Shane nearly did it then. He wanted to turn around, cry, tell Jesse he loved him more than anything. He tried to turn, but his body was stuck. He couldn't move.

"Jess, I love you. I'd do anything to take it back."

"Too late."

Shane felt a piercing, tearing pain in the center of his spine.

"You ripped me in half, Shane. It's your turn…."

Shane woke and sat up with a gasp, holding a hand

against his chest to stanch the river of blood he could still feel flowing from his ribs. The slicing agony of the knife was an aching memory on his skin. He felt sweaty and cold at the same time, and his heart crashed painfully.

He fucking stabbed me. What the hell, Jesse?

Shane looked over at Kayden, resting and pale in the silvery moonlight from the open balcony curtains. *It was a dream. Just a fucked-up fucking dream.*

It started the same as it had for years—with Jesse's face crumpling in pain as Shane, the elected messenger, broke the news that their new label didn't like Jesse's look and planned to replace him before Luck laid down their first tracks. And, what was worse, they asked Shane to step forward as lead singer. He'd known that would be the hardest part to tell. But, shit, *was* there an easy way to tear out somebody's heart?

Shane blinked in the partial darkness of Kayden's room. He could still hear Jesse's voice as the dream replayed in his head, as thick with tears as it had been on that day. God, what a horrible nightmare. He'd never been one to believe that dreams meant something, but this time felt more real than ever, as if he were reliving that moment all over again. Except for the ending. Who knew what the hell *that* was about? Probably just his conscience fucking with him, now that he was trying to move on. Not that Shane would ever forget. Even if he never saw Jesse again.

Shit, Jess. Wherever you are, I'm sorry. I've said it a million times, but I am so, so sorry.

"Hey, what's wrong?" Kayden's sleepy voice startled him.

"Nothing," Shane muttered quickly. "Sorry I woke you up."

"I was awake. Just thinking."

"'Bout what?"

"Oh, um, there's something I was planning to do while I was here in Chicago. I'm starting to think it's a bad idea, though."

"How come?"

Kayden shrugged. "Best laid plans, you know? You should go back to sleep."

Shane searched his expression, trying to read something, anything, on that inscrutable face. He settled back down against his pillow and reached out to draw Kayden to his side. Surprisingly, Kayden didn't protest but nestled himself in and made a small humming noise.

They were quiet for a few minutes. Shane could tell Kayden was awake too. He wasn't sure if he was going to be able to fall back to sleep after that awful dream. *Jesse. Why are you coming back to me now, when I could finally be happy for once?* He gritted his teeth and fought to keep from squeezing Kayden.

"Hey, Shane?"

Shane was surprised to hear his voice. "Yeah?"

"Can I ask you a question?"

"Sure."

"How come you don't still know your best friend—the guy from your tattoo?"

Shane bit back a sigh. Jesse was the last thing he wanted to talk about, especially with Kayden. "We got in a fight. Like I said, it was a long time ago."

"But didn't you ever want to find him and apologize? Make up or whatever?"

Yes. Find him and apologize, tell him I still loved him, that I'd take it all back if I could. But it would've never worked. Jesse hated me after that day.

"It wasn't worth it," was all Shane said. He didn't know

how else to tell Kayden how hopeless the cause would've been.

"You never even tried?"

Shane shook his head, glad that Kayden couldn't see the misery on his face. "Look, I fucked up, okay? I gave up when I should've fought, and I walked away when I should've stayed." He paused. A bitter laughed escaped him before he could fight it back. "It's all anyone in my family ever does."

"But what if he was looking for you?"

"Trust me, he wasn't. Listen, Jesse's ancient history, all right? He doesn't matter anymore. Can we just go to sleep?"

"Yeah," Kayden answered. His voice sounded thick, like he was holding back a yawn or something. Poor guy was probably exhausted.

"Night, Kayden."

"Night."

SHANE WOKE AGAIN when the room was flooded with early-morning light. He reached over to ask Kayden to close the curtains—they were on his side after all—but all he found was an empty pillow. It was warm from the sun, so Shane couldn't tell how long Kayden had been gone. *Maybe he needed coffee or something. I'll just wait.* He waited, and waited... and waited. Nearly an hour passed, and Kayden didn't return. Nausea started to build in the bottom of Shane's stomach. Had he fucked things up by sleeping with Kayden too soon?

He hoped maybe Kayden was just feeling awkward, or perhaps he needed some time to think things through. Shane dragged himself out of bed, wishing he could stay, wishing Kayden was there with him. Oddly enough, even though it was Kayden who was making him stress, he was also the only person Shane wanted to go to for comfort. He knew he was in big trouble.

Shane collected his scattered clothes from the floor of the opulent room. He hadn't noticed the expensive silk wallpaper the night before, or the gorgeous oriental rugs. He hadn't noticed anything but the taste of Kayden's skin and how perfect he felt with Kayden inside him.

Dressing reminded him of the fact that there had been a man inside of him the night before. Shane was sore; his body ached from the new stretch. But he didn't mind. It was almost as if he could still feel Kayden. He wanted to feel him again and again. In every way possible. Shane was reluctant to leave the room. He felt like a kid waiting for a crush, hoping the other person felt the same way. No, not a crush. More. A lot more. He wasn't sure what words he'd be willing to put on it quite yet, but....

Shane searched the room until he found a little pad of hotel paper and a pen.

K—

I'll see you tonight. ~~Waited around a~~ *Just wanted to say good morning, and I hope you have a good day.*

—Shane

He wanted to say so much more. *Where are you? I wanted to wake up kissing and touching. I wanted to hold you.* Shane felt like such a sap. What had happened to the rock star? He glanced around, making sure he had everything he needed, then slipped out and headed back to his room to shower alone. It was the last thing he wanted to do.

Hours later, Shane was walking into the greenroom before his concert, nervous as hell. He'd passed the point of wondering hours earlier. There was something wrong. He hadn't heard from Kayden all day. Not a text, not a call, not a "hey, nice fucking you last night." Nothing. And Shane was about to see him. He was petrified.

Shane gingerly pushed the door open, halfway expecting Kayden not to be there after what Oliver and Surya had said about him going off and doing his own thing before every concert. Part of him hoped the room would be empty. He wasn't sure if he was ready to face the music. He didn't know what he would do if Kayden completely rejected him. *If? More like* when. *God.* Shane knew if he didn't throw up right there from nerves and everything else that was tying him up in knots, it would be a fucking miracle.

Kayden was there, seated on one of the couches, sipping from a cup of hot tea and tapping his foot to whatever song played on his phone. Shane took a deep breath and approached him warily.

"Uh, Kayden?" He hated the insecurity in his voice.

Kayden removed his ear pieces and gave Shane a bored look. "Yes?"

"I waited for you this morning. What happened to you?" *Shit, I sound pathetic.*

Kayden shrugged. "I went to the gym. Then I did some work on my new piano piece."

"Why didn't you wake me up to say good-bye?" Shane leaned closer and reached out. He wanted to touch, kiss, anything to recapture the intimacy they shared less than twenty-four hours before. Kayden flinched away.

"What for? You didn't think last night was anything... important, did you?"

"*Yeah.*" It came out as a whisper.

Bile rose in Shane's throat. He couldn't believe what

was happening. It was a nightmare. Worse, though, because there was no escape. Even now, all he wanted was to feel Kayden's mouth on his again. Kayden, who gave him a nonchalant eyebrow raise, as if to say, *what's your problem?*

"I should think that you of all people would understand casual fucking." The words were even worse than that look.

"But that's not what last night was—not what I want. Not from you."

Shane could've sworn that Kayden flinched, but then the cool mask slid back into place.

"Then I guess you'll have to get it somewhere else from now on." Kayden shrugged again and got to his feet. When Shane didn't move immediately, he pointed at the doors. "If you don't mind, my band is going on. I need to get around you."

Kayden put his earbuds in as if he were dismissing the entire conversation. Then he ducked under Shane's arm and walked away toward the stage door, like nothing gut-wrenching and earth-cracking had just happened.

Shane didn't know if he wanted to watch Moonlight, if he could stand to even *look* at Kayden right then, but he couldn't stand *not* to watch either. Kayden was an addiction —obviously an unhealthy one, but Shane wasn't ready to shake him. He wasn't ready to give up either. When he heard the roar of the crowd, his decision was made. Heart still heavy, Shane wandered up to the side of the stage where he could watch until it was time for him to prep for his own performance.

They were fantastic—even more so than usual. Or maybe Shane was just seeing everything he felt last night in Kayden's eyes, feeling the throbbing desire in his lyrics. It was all there, in gorgeous complex harmony—love, lust, pain, happiness. Shane wanted so badly to be the person

Kayden was singing about, singing to. He stood rapt, not caring if it was time for him to go warm up himself.

Kayden was preparing for his piano ballad. It usually came after "Black Heart" and before their encore. Shane knew he needed to get downstairs, but he had to stay for this one last song. The ballad killed him every time. It was beautiful, melancholy—wait, what was Kayden doing? Instead of sitting at the shiny concert grand, he pulled out a stool and his acoustic. Did he have some new material?

"So, everyone, you'll be the first to hear this song." The arena went nuts. Of course they did. Exclusive new Moonlight material? Even Shane couldn't help grinning. "I started writing it ages ago. You'll have to forgive me. I was a bit dramatic when I was a kid." He gave the crowd one of those unassuming, sunny smiles. They ate it up. There were claps and whistles as Kayden settled in and strummed a few chords on his guitar.

Then he began. The song started in B minor, the chords picked out in a complicated three-four rhythm. Then it switched to G, with the same gorgeously complex picking rhythm. Shane smiled. The chords and that strumming pattern sounded strangely familiar. He liked—

"Second glances,

warmed from the sun,"

Shane's breath stuck in his throat. *Wh—how?* It was impossible. His heart, which had already been racing with excitement, started slamming against his ribs. *Slam! Jesse.... Slam! Kayden.... Slam! It can't fucking be real.*

"Moments slow passing,

never done."

It was real. Nobody knew that song. *Nobody.* It had only ever been between him and Jesse, and they never even finished it. Kayden glanced over to where he stood just offstage. Their eyes met, and Shane's stomach heaved. He was reeling and in shock, so close to blackout panic that the edges of his vision had started to blur.

"For the first time,
Someone sees who I am...."

Shane slid down the support beam he was leaning up against until he hit the ground. He trapped his head between his knees. *Breathe.... Breathe.* Shane didn't know how to process it. Did Kayden know Jesse? Was this all some kind of fucking joke? Mess with the dumb rock star—God, were Kayden and Jesse *together?* And then Shane remembered that moment in the limo when Kayden laughed and covered his mouth with his hand—and he did it again in Rome when they took cover from the rain.

Exactly the way Jesse used to.

There was no fucking way. Not a single feature on Kayden Berlin's perfect face looked like his Jesse.

"And I can't let you slip through my hands."

Kayden's voice rang out, throaty and beautiful... and so familiar, Shane wanted to curl up and die. How could he have missed that all these months? Shane felt like he was going to vomit. Even if nothing else seemed familiar, that voice was Jesse.

"So hold me closer, never push me away...."

Shane was locked in place, hypnotized by Kayden's—no, Jesse's voice—his words, the still unbelievable reality that it really was his best friend, his first love, up there on the stage. How could he not have known? It was so *obvious* now that he knew what to look for. Jesse had finished his guitar solo and was bridging into the next verse.

"You made me suffer,
Tore me in two...."

The disbelieving joy that had been slowly blossoming in Shane died.

"When you told me, I wasn't good enough for you.
No grand gestures, or well-practiced lines....
Will make me less bitter, or you less unkind...."

Shane's stomach clenched; the nausea that had been threatening all evening rose in a wave. No more. He had to get out. Get the fuck out. Get as far away from everybody as he could. He wanted to run and run until nothing looked like the horrible, surreal mess that his life had become. He sat there drowning in it, unable to move, unable to process anything beyond his shock.

After a moment, he forced himself to stand, ready to take off, ready to ditch everything. But when he turned, Nick was there with his guitar, holding it out to him.

"C'mon. Quit trying to crawl up Berlin's ass. We've gotta warm up. Practice room upstairs?"

"The greenroom sounds better," Dre added from his position behind Nicky.

The greenroom. Kayden, no, Jesse—*Jesse*—would be there after his performance. Shane couldn't see him. Couldn't be in the same hemisphere.

"Upstairs," he croaked. "Let's go before the stage crew tramples us."

Shane didn't know how he was going to get through the rest of the night, or the next day. Or any day for that matter.

He felt like he was going to die.

CHAPTER TEN

Jesse Seider, known to most people by his stage name, Kayden Berlin, slumped against the door of his dressing room and tried to get his racing heartbeat under control.

The second he and the others had come off stage after their encore, it felt like a fifteen-ton truck had dropped onto his chest. Suddenly, he couldn't breathe, couldn't swallow, couldn't even *think* clearly.

He made his excuses and escaped to Moonlight's dressing room instead of following Surya and Ollie in their quest to get drinks. They didn't notice he was clinging to control by the tips of his fingernails, trying desperately not to break down in front of the roadies who rushed past them to start prepping the stage for Luck.

The confident, unruffled mask of Kayden Berlin protected him once again. But there, in the relative quiet of their dressing room, that mask was gone.

God. Oh God.

What had he done? Shane's face, that broken, agonized expression, that shattered look the moment he heard the song and recognized Jesse for who he truly was... Jesse would never forget it. And only then, in that instant, had Jesse realized just how badly he'd fucked everything up.

Why didn't I just talk to him?

Why had he let the petty need for some kind of revenge overrule his common sense? What was that old phrase? Two wrongs didn't make a right. Cliché as it was, the truth of the words hit Jesse hard. Shane hurt him all those years ago. Nearly destroyed him. But the smug self-satisfaction he'd expected to feel when he finally paid Shane back for all that pain—it was more than a little conspicuous in its absence. There was no sense of victory. He hadn't won a goddamn thing. In fact, the strongest emotion ringing through him right then, clear as a bell, was loss.

He'd done an awful thing. Terrible. A thing the younger version of himself would have never done to someone he cared about. To Shane. Especially not to Shane.

Jesse fisted a hand in his hair and groaned. His clothes clung to him, soaked with sweat from his performance and the heat of the stage lights, chafing his sensitized skin. *Oh God.* He had to fix it. But how? How could he possibly make this better? Had he made it so Shane wouldn't be able to go onstage with Luck and perform?

What the hell was I thinking? He hadn't been. Not really. His emotions had been in control, not his head. His pain from the night before, from Shane's dismissal of Jesse to Kayden. He'd been reconsidering his plan before that moment, thinking maybe in the morning he would explain and they could talk. But then Shane admitted he'd never gone after Jesse, said that Jesse was ancient history. Didn't matter anymore. And how could he not go through with it then? He had his pride, after all.

Still, hurt pride or not, it was wrong. *He'd* been wrong.

Now the person he wanted most was probably lost to him. If Jesse tried to apologize, no doubt Shane would slam him down. But he had to try anyway. He couldn't leave it like this. He couldn't stand it.

Jesse sucked in a trembling breath and straightened away from the door. What was he doing, cowering in the dressing room? He had to go back out there, make sure Shane was okay, show his support in some way. Show Shane that, hell, Jesse didn't even know what. But he had to do *something*. And then later he could find Shane and explain. Apologize. Maybe things weren't as hopeless as he feared. Maybe Shane would understand. Maybe....

But if *maybes* were water, he could fill a lake to drown in. He couldn't let himself go down that path. Because the biggest maybe of all was the hope that he hadn't hurt Shane too much for their relationship to recover. Any relationship, even just friendship. That maybe would crush him if it turned out to be wrong.

Jesse checked his appearance in the mirror across the room. His hair was mussed, his eyes too bright, but aside from that, the same coolly beautiful face he'd grown accustomed to over the years after his surgeries stared back at him.

He'd thought once that beauty was all he wanted. All he needed to get over Shane. Blue Horizon hadn't liked his look? He'd changed everything, hoping to never face that kind of rejection again. But now he felt a moment of regret for the old Jesse. Plain, loyal, dorky Jesse, who would've never treated his best friend so cruelly. Deep inside, that boy wasn't entirely gone. No matter how much Jesse might like to think otherwise.

He owed his best friend more than hiding back here. Even if Shane had never apologized to *him*. Even if Shane never forgave what Jesse had done. Jesse wouldn't forgive *himself* unless he tried.

SHANE STUMBLED onto the dark stage still in shock. It had been nearly impossible to make it through warm-up with the others. He'd seen Nick watching him, concerned, but he didn't even know where to begin.

Nicky had never even known what Jesse was to him. Shane had no idea how he was going to make it through their set, which had to be amazing, since it was their hometown arena. His throat was tight and aching from holding back the tide of tears and emotions and everything else trying to well up from inside him.

He still couldn't believe it was Jesse. That Jesse had been there, right under his nose, the entire damn time. *Why didn't he just tell me?*

Shane understood the dramatics, he supposed, even if they didn't seem very much like something the Jesse he knew would have done. And why point out so cruelly that he was on top, the better musician, the one who hadn't washed out? He'd always been the best of them, even at the very beginning. There was no doubt about that. But it was too late to think about it. The lights blew on with the strength of the sun, and Nick's muscular bass started the opening chords for their cover of "London Calling." They'd been playing it during the tour as a tribute to Moonlight.

Shane closed his eyes and tried to get lost in the music, in the discordant tones and driving rhythm of The Clash's old anthem. They segued from that into their newest hit single effortlessly. Shane was finally finding his groove, forgetting the real world and living for the stage. This one hour was his reprieve before he had to go back to dealing with Jesse and him and Kayden and the tangled ball of mess that they were together.

He played like his guitar was on fire, growling lyrics into the mic and giving his all to the dirty little show he put on with his bandmates. As improbable as even he would've thought, Shane had to say it was one of their best shows. He could see Nick's grin, feel the energy from the others onstage, drown in the force reflected from their fans shouting and screaming in the crowd—and he was himself once again.

Until he glanced over at Nick and saw Jesse standing in the wings, watching him perform.

Shane tried not to falter. He had to struggle to keep his strumming on beat, to remember a word of the lyrics he'd penned himself. Jesse smiled for a moment, seeming strangely encouraging and supportive... and it helped. Like it always had. That smile, when he managed to view the rare uncovered version, was one of the only things that made Shane feel like everything could be okay. In that moment, he felt a small bubble of euphoria that swelled and overwhelmed all the bad feelings and the weirdness. He had his best friend back. The boy he'd loved for more than eleven years was a man, and he wasn't lost anymore. He was only twenty feet away....

But he hated Shane. He'd said so in front of thousands of people less than thirty minutes ago. And he was looking at Shane with sadness in his eyes, like he was saying good-bye, like he was saying sorry. And just like that, the good feelings were gone.

Fuck good-bye. Jesse had no right to lay something like that on him and then act like it was over. They weren't done yet. Fuck sorry while he was at it too. All those weeks. He could've said something. What he'd done was awful, unfor-givable.

Shit. Don't let him ruin tonight any more than he already has.

Shane wrenched his eyes away from Jesse and focused on the music, the crowd, his grinning bandmates. *This is it. My chance to take my fading star and make it shine again. Show Jesse I'm not the loser he keeps saying I am.* He put everything he had into that show—to forget, or maybe to remember how good it used to feel. Their fans loved it, cheering them through four encore songs until they finally left the stage sweaty, worn, and—for at least most of the members of Luck—smiling from ear to ear.

Nick clapped him on the back as soon as they entered the momentary quiet of the greenroom. "You fuckin' rocked tonight, bro. We were awesome."

"Yeah, man. I'll drag Berlin's ass up to the stage and tie him there every night if it makes you play like that." Dre was grinning and sweating and sticking his hand out for a high five.

Shane tiredly complied, giving his brother and one of his oldest friends a smile. "Hey, listen, guys. I think I'm going to head back to the hotel. I can't party after that. I feel like I ran a damn marathon."

"That's 'cause you're old," Nick said with a snort.

"Yeah, whatever. Have fun tonight. Do everything I wouldn't do. Twice."

Nick and Dre laughed and bumped fists. Shane went off in search of Em so he could get some anonymous trans-port back to the hotel. The last thing he needed in his current mental state was to run into a bunch of fans.

• • •

THE SILENCE of his hotel room was a relief after all the chaos in the last couple of hours. Shane sank onto his bed fully clothed and stared at the bank of windows that looked out onto Chicago's lights. *What a hellfuck of a night.* Adrenaline from the concert fading, he finally got to take a good look at how he felt about the whole crazy thing. Kayden was *Jesse.*

God. How could anyone have known? How could he have not seen? Shane thought about all the little comments that he made, especially the one about the tattoo being his best friend's initials, and he felt stupid. So fucking stupid. And God, all those times he practically threw himself at Berlin, begged to be let into his perfect little pants. It was humiliating, and it hurt. He'd actually had Jesse *inside* his body, and the bastard didn't seem to feel it was necessary to tell the truth even then.

No wonder he was trying to avoid talking to me last night. Shane realized Jesse must have been planning the stunt he pulled earlier for months. *Did he plan last night too? Was the revenge fuck part of it—to let me know who was on top?*

Shane wished he knew what to feel. No, that wasn't true. He felt a lot of things. Mad, hurt, mortified beyond repair. And to think he had to get up in the morning and look at Jesse's smug, better-than-you face and hear him talk in that *dumb*, fake English accent.

Fuck.

Shane wasn't sure if he could do it—look at Jesse day after day for another three months. And he didn't know what would be worse, the asshole version of Kayden or the apologetic version he'd seen earlier. The one who gave him a look that said "I know I just fucked up your world. My bad." Fuck Jesse Seider. Fuck Kayden Berlin. Fuck them both.

He ripped his shirt off and threw it to the floor. His jeans were harder to get off. Sweat and tight denim didn't exactly make for an easy dramatic removal. When he finally wrestled them to the ground, Shane stomped off toward the shower, hoping to scrub the disgusting feeling of the night off his skin. The shower helped a little, he supposed. At least he didn't smell like the sweat of his entire band anymore. The hot water didn't erase that face from his mind, though—that perfect, gorgeous, *hateful* face.

Shane dried off and pulled on a pair of loose old sweats to sleep in. Hopefully he'd be able to. Shane rolled himself up in the blankets, nice and tight like he used to when he was afraid of lightning storms in the summer. He squeezed his eyes shut and tried to picture anything other than Jesse's face. It was impossible. He kept comparing Kayden, the ice queen with the perfectly sculpted cheeks and delicate nose, to the awkward and lovable Jesse from his memory. If it weren't for the voice and the eyes that were the wrong color but the exact right shape, then Shane would have thought it was impossible, no matter what song Kayden knew or what little gestures he had that seemed familiar.

The only thing Shane *did* know was that he couldn't look that little shit in the face again. Ever. Not after what he'd done. No answers, no truths were worth the crushing humiliation and hurt that he felt every time he thought about the fact that Jesse had been with him for three months, playing petty games and never *once* revealing who he was. Shane decided he was going to pack up his shit in the morning and go home. Fuck the consequences.

He was done.

· · ·

Shane was woken several hours later by a soft knock on the door. At first, he wasn't sure he even heard it. But then a second quiet knock convinced him that he hadn't dreamed it. He glanced at the clock. It was still the middle of the night. Who could be knocking on his door?

Oh shit. What if it's Jesse?

He struggled out of bed and pulled on a T-shirt. It was a long stumble in the dark. Shane didn't even give himself a chance to decide if he wanted to open the door or not. He cracked it just a few inches to find Nick on the other side.

You're not disappointed that it's Nicky.

And he wasn't. Shane *didn't* want Jesse to come and try to explain himself. Did he? The nauseated ache in his stomach came back immediately. No. He didn't. Not yet, anyway. Maybe not ever.

"Hey, Nicky," Shane said quietly. He flipped on the light switch and scooted aside to let his brother in.

"Dude, you okay? You looked kinda shitty earlier. I was worried."

"Thanks." Shane gave Nick a wry smile. "I'm not sure if I'm okay, actually."

"Did Berlin do something to you?" Nick's pugnacious face was perfectly in character.

Shane let out a small, sad laugh. "You have no idea."

"You want me to fuck him up for you?"

"No. That wouldn't help anything." *Although it might be entertaining right about now.*

"So what, Shaney?"

"I think I need to go home for a while."

"Hey, that's cool. We've got a week after the Pittsburgh concert."

"No, I meant more like tomorrow."

Nick froze. Shane knew exactly what he was thinking.

It would be the same thing on Shane's mind if Nick decided to up and leave.

"Uh, you can't. Like, really, you can't. We're on the road to Cleveland in the morning."

"I know, but I need out. After tonight—"

"What the fuck did that *asswipe* do to you? If you're going to even talk about ruining everything, you better start giving me some fucking answers."

"You wouldn't believe me if I told you."

"Spit it out, bro." Nick held up his hand. "Wait, are we talking, like, rape or something here? Because I'm not sure I can hear about that."

"No, moron. He didn't rape me. That would imply I had any intention of saying no."

"Dude, you let him fuck you? You never—"

Shane held up his own hand. "That's not it, Nicky. He's Jesse."

Nick sputtered out a laugh. "What the hell are you talking about?"

"Kayden Berlin is *Jesse*."

"I didn't see you doing any drugs at the concert. Please tell me you're not nuts. We seriously don't have time for you to be nuts."

"No, he's Jesse. Listen, you know that song Kayden was playing when you came to get me?"

"The acoustic one?"

"Yeah. Nicky, *Jesse* wrote that song—with me when we were kids. We're the only two people who ever heard it. Ever."

"But Kayden is super hot. There's no fucking way he's dorky-ass Jesse."

"I thought so too for a second, like maybe he knew Jesse somehow, and he'd gotten the lyrics... but then I realized it had to be him. He does this thing with his hand when he smiles where he covers his mouth. Remember that? When he's not trying to be Kayden, he still does it. And even with the accent, there's this thing that he says." Shane found himself smiling and shook himself out of it. "It's him. I know it is."

"So he sang that song to tell you he's *Jesse?*" Nick snorted. "Sorry, man. I'm still having a hard time believing this shit."

"Yeah, the song told me he was Jesse. It's true."

"So what's the big problem here? Berlin is Jesse. You fucked. I'm guessing you liked it. Let's get on with the show."

"Did you hear the lyrics? About how he was bitter and no matter what I do, it'll never be enough for him to forgive me? And all that after he *fucked* me? I can't look at him again."

Nick's face tightened. "You promised me. You said that you'd be cool and whatever happened with Berlin wouldn't wreck our tour."

"That was before I knew 'Berlin' was Jesse! Can't you see how that's different?"

"I don't care who he is. Even if Kayden Berlin was fucking *Santa Claus*, I still don't want this damn tour fucked up over your little thing with him."

Shane went cold. "That's the problem, Nicky, isn't it?"

"What?"

"You don't care. You *never* cared."

"What the hell are you talking about?"

"When you guys decided to jump at kicking Jess out of the band, did you ever consider how I might have felt about it?"

"God, you're so gay. Why on earth could you possibly

have had feelings about that? Yeah, it sucked, but oh well. That's the business."

"I had feelings about it because I was in *love* with him, you asshole. Was, am, have been for years...." Shane's voice trailed off.

Nick choked. "You were in love with *Jesse?*"

"Yeah. And that face you just made right there is the reason why I never told you. You guys fucked it all up when you made me do that to him."

"Hey! Don't pin your shit on me. You could've told me back then."

"And would you have listened?"

"Ye—" Nick made a face. "Maybe. I don't know. But you didn't even try. Doesn't sound like you loved him all that much."

"You know what? Fuck you. You ruined everything for me back then. Maybe it's my turn. Get the hell out of my room. I'm done with this."

He shoved Nick toward the door.

"Done with what?"

"This conversation, this tour, the band, Kayden Berlin, Jesse fucking Seider. Fuck it all."

"I can't fucking *believe* you're doing this," Nick shouted as he threw the door open and stomped into the hall. He turned like he had something else to say, but the limit of Shane's patience had officially been reached.

"Believe it." Shane slammed the door on his brother's outraged face.

He wasn't waiting for morning, when he'd have to talk to Em, to his agent, to all the people he didn't want to deal with. Shane was leaving right then and there. He flew to the closet and dragged out two suitcases, bumping his bare toe and swearing before he unzipped them and slung them open onto the champagne-colored carpet. Fuck Nicky. He didn't give a shit what his brother thought. He was getting the hell out.

Shane jerked open one of the drawers on the expensive hotel dresser, caring only at the last second that he didn't tear the damn thing off its perfectly oiled runners. The last thing he needed was a huge bill from the hotel, seeing as though he was probably going to be out some major money in the next few weeks if his label decided to cause trouble.

He did feel a little bad. Yeah, he would kind of be screwing Luck by leaving, but they could get along without him. There were a million guitarists who knew their songs backward and forward, and Nicky's voice wasn't all that different from his own.

Shane just wanted to go home, get somewhere he felt safe, and stay there. Forever. He dumped the contents of the drawers into his suitcases, not bothering to fold anything. Then he went to the closet and yanked the few things he had off the hangers and slung them on top of the mound of clothing already there.

There was another knock on his door, softer this time. Shane wanted to scream or cry or maybe break some shit against the wall rock-star style. Instead he just pressed on his eyes, trying to get rid of the raging headache that had plagued him since he left the arena.

Fuck.

He kept thinking he was used to it. Not over it, probably never over it, but at least getting acclimated to the idea that Jesse, *Jesse*, had been with him the whole time, and he hadn't known. How the hell had he not known? If someone asked, Shane would've said he'd recognize Jesse anywhere. And maybe he had, deep in his heart.

The knock came again. Even softer this time. Hesitant.

"I haven't slashed my wrists yet, Nicky. Just leave me alone, okay?"

Shane sighed and ran a hand through his hair. He pulled it a little as if maybe that would get rid of the pounding headache, the awful flashes where he remembered the moment that he realized Kayden was his Jesse. And truthfully he wasn't even surprised. Shocked, maybe, but the second he knew it was Jesse, Shane *knew*. All of a sudden Kayden felt so achingly familiar. And that was what hurt the most. Because the part of Kayden he'd fallen for *was* Jesse. It was the shy smile and the endearing insecurity. It wasn't Kayden Berlin he'd been wanting at all. It was Jesse. And Jesse wasn't ever—

"It's not Nick, Shane. It's me. Jesse."

Fuck. Jesse was right outside his door. Fuck. Like, really. *Fuck.* Shane froze. He didn't know what the hell to do. It was everything he dreamed of for years, but it was such a mess.

"Shane, I know you're in there. Can you please open the door?" He sounded so much like *him* in that moment that Shane found himself crossing the thick carpet and reaching for the handle.

When Shane opened it, he sucked in a hard breath and nearly choked on it. Jesse's hair was still standing up, thick with products from the stage, but Shane could tell he'd hastily washed his face and put on a pair of faded jeans, ratty Converse, and a simple black T-shirt. It was Jesse. All that was left of Kayden were those stupid green contacts and his thin body.

"J-Jess." Shane didn't know what to say. He was still so, so angry and hurt and torn apart and more shocked than he'd ever been in his life. He didn't know what the fuck to do with all the emotions that were drowning him. He felt like his lungs were about to collapse.

Shane took a few steps back, trying to get some space. Jesse followed. "Hey, Shane. Feels like it's been forever, huh?"

And for some reason that snapped Shane out of it. "You *asshole*. All summer. All fucking summer you've pretended to be someone else. Then you go up on that stage and pretty much tell the whole fucking crowd that you hate my guts and now you're *here*? Get the fuck out."

"*Shane*. I'm sorry. Can we talk? Please?"

"About what? You wanna tell me you hate me again? 'Cause I'm pretty goddamn sure it sunk in the first time."

"I need—"

"You need what?" Shane raked another angry hand through his hair. "You know what, never mind. I don't want to know. I don't want to hear about what you need. I don't *care* what you need. Not anymore. I'm outta here." He slammed his suitcases closed, zipped them up, and yanked his jacket on.

"But you can't just leave—"

"Yes, I fucking can." Shane took a deep breath, hauled the strap for his guitar case over his shoulder, then pulled out the retractable handles on his suitcases without looking back at Jesse. "Don't follow me. I can't talk to you."

He wheeled his bags to the door and jerked it open from where it had drifted closed after Jesse fucking Seider walked back into his life again. He stalked out into the hallway, away from the sound of Jesse calling his name, away from everything.

He had more stuff on the tour bus ready to go the next day, but whatever it was, he decided he could live without it. Even his favorite electric. God, that sucked. But he wasn't going to try to go after the thing.

The night concierge seemed a bit shocked to see him, but hopped to it when Shane asked what she could do about getting him a seat on the next flight to New York. She worked whatever computer magic desk jockeys are so amazing at, then smiled and told him he had a seat on the flight that left at six that morning.

It gave him just two hours to get to the airport and through security. Perfect. No time to think until he was already on the plane headed for home.

He gratefully accepted the concierge's offer to call him a limo, which he waited for quietly until she told him it had arrived. A part of him expected Jesse to reappear, but he didn't. Shane was glad. Really, he was. He wasn't looking around the corner for a tiny irritating pixie in old jeans and a ratty pair of Chucks. Jesse could go fuck himself. Everyone could. Shane was done with the whole damn mess.

So with no fanfare, no lights, nothing but his suitcases and the guitar on his back, Shane Ventura left Chicago, his band, and everything he knew behind.

CHAPTER ELEVEN

New York

THE INCESSANT KNOCKING ON SHANE'S DOOR HAD moved beyond the distracting stage and gone straight into *absolutely fucking annoying.*

Shane ignored it anyway, as he had with just about everything over the past week. Phone calls, text messages, e-mails—he hadn't responded to any of them. Em left him multiple voice mails, some pleading, some enraged. In the last one, he went off on a tangent about lawsuits and breach of contract.

Shane deleted the message without even a flicker of hesitation. So what if the record label sued him? He didn't give a shit. After over a decade in a multiplatinum-selling band, he had money to spare. Shane Ventura was many things, but he wasn't a complete moron. He'd done his best to ensure that he would never wind up back in some poor, shitty neighborhood again, no matter what happened with Luck. He'd put a good chunk of his money into the hands of a reputable investment firm and convinced Nick to do the same.

He could survive Blue Horizon's wrath, and the reality was that the label couldn't afford to lose a band like Luck, not with their massive fan base. They'd fight Shane for a while, and then they'd probably fire his ass and replace him. He didn't think the rest of the band would suffer, except for maybe some embarrassment. But at that point, he was almost beyond caring, and the very last thing he wanted to do was talk about the fucking tour or Moonlight. *Especially* Moonlight.

Shane knew he was being stupid. He had become the poster boy for depression. Sulking around his condo in his pajamas, overeating, and alternating between action movies and episodes of the TV shows he recorded on his DVR. Might as well stick him in an ad for antidepressants.

But he didn't have the slightest idea how to deal with the emotional fallout from the stunt Kayden—no, *Jesse*—had pulled. His heart had been broken before, when he walked away from Jesse all those years ago. It was broken again, this time *because* of Jesse. Hell, maybe it hadn't even fully recovered in the first place. That would explain why he'd never been able to let Jesse's memory go.

The pounding at the door continued. Shane sighed and set aside the half-empty tray of *arroz con dulce* he'd been picking at. There was a Puerto Rican restaurant around the corner from his building, and most of his recent takeout orders had come from them. He'd ordered his favorite dish— sirloin steak with caramelized onions over white rice—twice in the past three days, and he was on his fourth pan of the rice pudding. It was comfort food, plain and simple. The only fond memories he had from his childhood were of his mom's cooking, especially when she went all-out around the holidays. His father never cooked. Once Shane's mother took off, they lived on frozen pizza, mac 'n' cheese, and premade dinners.

"Fuck off!" he yelled in the general direction of the foyer.

The banging paused briefly and then redoubled. Whoever was out there was a persistent fucker, Shane would give him that. He'd laid into the doorbell for a good five minutes before he started on the whole knocking routine. No one else had stuck around that long, which meant it was probably Nick.

Shane sighed again and got to his feet. By his estimate, Luck and Moonlight had probably just started the week-long break between the Pittsburgh concert and the one in New York the following Friday. He could only ignore his brother for so long.

They hadn't spoken since the argument in Chicago, though Nick had sent him over a dozen irate text messages, alternately calling him a selfish asshole and telling him to man up and stop being such a fucking chick. Nick didn't understand. He likely never would. As far as Shane knew, he'd never been in love, maybe not even in *like*, with anyone. Nick didn't think about things like relationships or commitment.

All he thought about was sex, drugs, and booze. Probably in that order too.

Shane trudged over to the door, toeing aside cardboard takeout containers and empty beer bottles. His condo was a disaster, but he'd kicked the maid out when she showed up to clean on Monday, and he hadn't been able to work up the motivation to do it himself. He wanted to wallow in his angst for a while longer before he decided just what the hell he was going to do—about Luck, about Jesse.

Part of Shane never wanted to see him again. Just the thought of that beautiful, flawless face twisted his stomach. He couldn't reconcile the idea of Jesse with Kayden in his mind, and when he tried, the pain and the betrayal made his head feel like it was going to explode. But another part of him still wanted Jesse, despite it all. And that hurt too. Maybe more than anything else.

When Shane reached the door, he didn't bother with the peephole, just unlocked it and pulled it open. The security in his building wouldn't let anyone through who wasn't on his list of approved guests, and there were only a handful of people allowed access to his floor.

"Look, Nicky, I already told you—"

The words died on his lips when he saw who stood in the hallway. It was Jesse, but not the aloof, glamorous rock star Shane had come to know. He was dressed much like Shane had seen him the last time, in dark-washed jeans, Chucks, and a navy blue hoodie. His pale blond hair was mussed, not in its usual sleek, forward comb. And as Jesse stared up at him, Shane realized his eyes weren't their customary sea green either. They were gray now, the color of steel.

Not Kayden Berlin's eyes. Jesse's.

Shane turned away from the door, unable to stand the sight of them. *Oh God.* He hadn't seen that color in so long. He'd forgotten how deeply it always affected him. Jesse's eyes had always been his best feature. As much as that calm, unwavering look Jesse used to give him when they were teenagers drove him crazy, he'd secretly loved having those eyes on him. Had ever since the moment he first saw Jesse without his glasses and the power of those eyes hit him full force in the solar plexus, knocking the breath right out of him.

"Can I come in?" Jesse's accent was gone.

No, not entirely gone, but barely there. A mild hint instead of the crisp British accent Shane was used to hearing.

Shane didn't answer. He headed toward his kitchen without looking back, knowing Jesse would follow. He hadn't been knocking at the door for over fifteen minutes without some kind of motive. Probably he'd been sent by the label to try to talk Shane into rejoining the tour.

Well, if that was the case, they made the wrong fucking call. Not that anyone else would have been able to convince him either, but having Jesse there was a blow, fuel on the fire of rage and pain that burned inside him. Nothing good could come of it.

"How did you get up here?" Shane asked when he heard Jesse step into the kitchen behind him. "They shouldn't have let you in."

"I bribed the security guard with an autograph for his daughter."

"I should have him fired."

"But you won't."

Shane opened the refrigerator and pulled out a beer. He turned to face Jesse as he twisted off the cap. "How do you know?"

"Because I know you." Jesse looked at him steadily. "That's not the type of person you are."

"You know me?" Shane sneered. "Yeah, maybe you do. Since I wasn't the one lying all this time. But apparently I don't know *you*. What should I even call you anyway? Is Kayden Berlin just a fucking act?"

"Not entirely. I am Kayden for the most part. But I'm Jesse too. Just not the same Jesse you used to know."

"That's for sure. The Jesse I knew would've never fucked me over like you did."

"Funny, but I used to think that same thing about you." Jesse crossed his arms across his chest and leaned back against the counter. "But then you did."

Shane swallowed, feeling sick. He set the beer bottle aside, no longer interested in drinking. Over the years, he'd often thought of what he might say if he ever saw Jesse again. He never imagined he would have the chance to actually apologize, and the speeches he'd mentally prepared flew right out of his head. So he said the first honest thing that came to mind instead.

"Yeah. And there hasn't been a day since that I haven't regretted it."

"You could have fooled me. You walked out of my life, never called me again. Never even showed any kind of remorse."

"So is that why you plotted this whole thing?" Shane asked, searching Jesse's face, which seemed both familiar and foreign at the same time. "Revenge?"

"Yes."

For a moment, Shane was taken aback. He hadn't expected Jesse to admit to it so readily. But he supposed there really wasn't any point in denying it. That little performance in Chicago said it all.

"I wanted you to see that you hadn't broken me," Jesse went on. "It's petty, I know, but I wanted to shove my success in your face. You can't imagine how I felt that day, when you walked away from me, like what we had meant nothing. Like *I* meant nothing."

Shane's stomach churned at the words, and he struggled to keep his face cool. He'd hurt Jesse, he knew. He'd never forgotten. *Would* never. But Jesse had more than gotten even. "And was *fucking* me part of your little scheme too?"

Jesse dropped his eyes. Shame flashed across his features. "No. I didn't mean for that to happen. The plan was just to make you want me, and I even tried to resist you that night. But when you kissed me, I couldn't stop myself. And I thought that if I was on top, if I was the dominant one, then I'd still be in control of the situation." He looked up and met Shane's gaze again, his gray eyes dark with remorse. "I'm sorry. It was stupid, and it was wrong. Sex was never supposed to be part of it, but I planned all along to reveal who I was in Chicago. In the beginning it seemed fitting."

Shane made a derisive noise. "Yeah, I bet. Fuck me over in the place where I did it to you."

Jesse's shamed look intensified. "Yeah," he said. "That was the plan. And I kept right on thinking it was a good one until I saw what it did to you. When I saw your face, saw the realization hit you, I knew how badly I'd messed things up. After all those years, all the resentment I felt toward you, I hadn't thought that hurting you would hurt me too."

Shane gave a disbelieving laugh and shook his head. "*You* were hurt? I thought you would've been happy. You got what you wanted, didn't you?"

"You remember that night in Chicago when I mentioned the best laid plans, don't you, Shane? Well, they never turn out the way you want them to." Jesse stepped closer, peering up into Shane's face, his expression earnest. "But I was furious with you because I loved you *so much*. And you chose a record deal over me. You let them kick me out of the band for such a shallow reason. You *left* me."

Shane didn't know what to say. He tried to hold on to his anger, but his thoughts were a jumbled mess. He stared at Jesse, so physically different from the boy Shane remembered, and then something from what Jesse had said finally struck him.

"Shallow reason," Shane repeated softly. "Is that why you did this to yourself? Changed the way you look? Because of what the label said?"

Jesse's eyes were sad. "I didn't want it to happen again."

"What did you have done?"

"Rhinoplasty. They did some work on my chin and jaw too, and I had Lasik surgery so I wouldn't need the glasses anymore."

"And the rest of it?" Shane gestured to Jesse's body.

Jesse smiled slightly. "I had a late growth spurt before I turned twenty. Grew a couple of inches. But the rest of it was hard work. I hooked up with a personal trainer, lost about thirty pounds. Then I dyed my hair and got some contacts, and Kayden Berlin was born."

"Why bother with the contacts if you didn't need them anymore?"

Jesse shrugged. "I thought the gray was too boring."

"Boring?" Shane repeated, incredulous. "Your eyes.... God. How could you not have known how gorgeous they are?"

"No one ever told me."

Shane opened his mouth to rectify that, to tell Jesse just how beautiful he always thought they were, how they'd always entranced him. But then he remembered himself. His anger. He snapped his mouth shut. *Don't be an asshole, Shane.*

"How did you wind up in England?" he asked, changing the subject to something else he'd been wondering.

"My dad got transferred through his job. He told me I

could stay behind and finish school here if I wanted, but you'd just kicked me out of the band. I thought anywhere else would be better than staying in Chicago."

"Why didn't you just forget about me?" Shane studied Jesse's face again. "Why even bother with all of this? You have Moonlight. You have everything you wanted now."

"I *couldn't* forget about you. Lord knows, I wanted to. But I couldn't. The hurt, it just never went away. So when I saw that both Luck and Moonlight had albums releasing around the same time, it seemed like the perfect opportunity. And I took it."

"Christ, Jess," Shane said without thinking, "I never forgot about you either. I loved you then. I just... I thought I was making the best decision to protect Nicky, to get him away from our father. But I hated hurting you. I hated it every fucking day. If I could take it all back, I would. It was the biggest mistake of my life, and I'm sorry. *So* sorry. You have no idea how I—" Shane's voice cracked and wavered. He swallowed hard. "All these years with Luck, they never felt right without you."

"You loved me then," Jesse said slowly, taking another step closer. "And now?"

"I...." Shane hesitated.

He wanted to say the words, to admit that he'd been falling fast and hard for Kayden Berlin, and a part of him loved Jesse as much now as he had back then. But how could he forgive what Jesse had done? How much of what they shared had been real, and how much had just been a part of Jesse's game?

Jesse finished closing the gap between them. His eyes were on the chain that still hung from Shane's throat, the one with the silver shamrock. Despite how pissed off he was, Shane hadn't been able to bring himself to remove it.

Jesse had given it to him as a present the day he graduated from high school, the first gift Shane had received from anyone since before his mother left. It'd hurt too much to try to let it go.

"I love you, Shane," Jesse said. And right then, there was nothing of Kayden Berlin in his voice or expression. The face was different, but it wasn't Moonlight's lead singer looking up at Shane. It was Jesse. Jesse with his heart and hope in his eyes. "Even as mad as I was at you, I don't think I ever stopped."

"Jess...."

"That night in Chicago, after we...." Jesse stopped, took a deep breath. "I watched you sleep for a while. I thought that in the morning, I'd confess everything, lay it all out there, and maybe we could forgive each other. But you woke up in the middle of the night, and I asked about your best friend, and you said—you said I didn't matter. And then I thought about that tattoo."

Jesse sighed and shook his head.

"The night before, it was such a turn-on, knowing you had my initials on you. But that morning, it just made me angry. I started to question *why* you'd done it. Was it just pity? Did you just feel sorry for poor, fat, ugly Jesse? How could you call me your best friend and then say I wasn't worth going after? And the next—"

"No, I didn't mean it like—"

"Please. Let me finish." Jesse swallowed thickly, his eyes on Shane's face. "The next thing I knew, I was walking out of that room, leaving you behind, and I decided to go through with my plan to sing that song. I shouldn't have done it. I should have gone with my instinct to just tell you everything. I should've asked you to explain. But I'm not very good at being rational where you're concerned. I lost my head."

Shane was quiet for a long moment; then he laughed dryly. "I haven't been very rational these last few months either. But about what I said that night, I didn't mean *you* weren't worth going after. I just—I didn't know how to approach you. I didn't think it was something you could ever forgive."

"You should have tried."

"I know. Fuck, do I know."

"But it doesn't matter anymore. We have a second chance now. We can start over." Jesse reached up and touched Shane's cheek, rasping his fingers over a few days' worth of stubble. Shane knew he probably looked like hell. Jesse didn't seem to mind. "I want to be with you. I never stopped wanting that."

Shane's breath caught; his heart squeezed painfully. Those were the words he would've killed to hear from Kayden Berlin only a couple of weeks before. But thinking about that made Shane remember something else, one last thing he needed to know. "What about those things you said? About how I'm a cliché? A train wreck?"

Jesse winced. "I just wanted to hurt you," he said, the words heavy with regret. "I couldn't stand the thought that you'd fallen into the trap so many people in this industry do. I know what you're capable of, Shane, and it's more than what you've been doing." Jesse paused. "And a part of me was jealous too. I hated seeing pictures of you with all those other men. Can you forgive me?"

Shane wanted to. *God*, how he wanted to. But it was too soon, the wounds too raw and fresh. "I don't know."

Jesse stepped back. For a second, he looked crushed and his mouth trembled, but he quickly smothered the expression. "I understand." He glanced to the right, at the clock display on the stove. "I should go. My flight leaves at four."

"Flight?"

"I'm going to London for a few days. I'll be back on Thursday."

Shane resisted the urge to grab Jesse, to haul him close and beg him to stay. The need to hold him, to kiss, to touch, was probably as strong as Shane's lingering anger. But he needed time to think, to process what Jesse had said.

"Have a good trip." It was all Shane could think to say without revealing too much.

"Thanks." Jesse gave him one last look and turned to go. He hesitated just outside the kitchen. "Shane, even if you can't forgive me, I hope you'll come back to the tour. Nick... he really needs you there."

Before Shane could respond, Jesse started moving again. A few seconds later, Shane heard his front door open and close. And then Jesse was gone.

JESSE RECLINED in his airplane seat and let his eyes drift shut as the flight attendants finished their announcements. He heard a few whispers of his name, Kayden Berlin, as some of his fellow passengers recognized him despite his attempts to disguise himself. He ignored the murmurs as best he could. He sure as hell didn't feel like the singer they so admired right now. Now after that scene with Shane. Jesse had never felt more like his awkward former self than when he was standing there in Shane's apartment, asking Shane to love him back—asking with everything he had.

Jesse's stomach twisted. What if it didn't work? They'd hurt each other so much, but Jesse's hurt was old. The sharp edges that used to cut into him were worn down by time.

Shane's hurt was fresh and painfully jagged. Jesse didn't know what he could do to make it go away. He was willing to try pretty much anything to undo what he'd done.

He wanted to call, text, email, stand outside Shane's apartment and shout his feelings until Shane really understood just how damn much Jesse still loved him. Would always love him. Shane was it for him. He knew it when they were kids, and he knew it with every guy he'd tried to replace Shane with. It worked to a point. Sort of. A cultured British accent didn't remind him of Shane's growly, street-tough voice. Well-heeled manners were the farthest thing from Shane's rough charm. So yeah, it had worked. Until they kissed him and, sure, it might have been hot, but it didn't feel *right*; or until he let them into his bed and a part of him always wished he hadn't.

That night in Chicago? That had felt so right it hurt. No part of him wanted out of Shane's bed. He just wanted to *touch* him and keep touching for the rest of his life, kiss him and never stop.

Jesse had to face the fact he might not get that chance.

It was a relief when his plane touched down in Heathrow in the gray near-light of an overcast early British morning. The seatbelt lights went off and Jesse struggled tiredly to his feet with the rest of the passengers. He texted his London driver, who was already in the queue at arrivals. Jesse was exhausted. He wanted his bed and some tea and a few hours of oblivion before he had to think of Shane's face again in that moment where he realized who Jesse was and it looked like his whole heart had burst open. Every time Jesse tried to close his eyes, it seemed that was all he saw.

Before leaving the plane, he made sure his hat covered

his shock of platinum hair and pulled up his hood for good measure. Might be a bit extreme, but Jesse wasn't in the mood to talk to anyone as he made his way through the airport. All he wanted was to sleep.

He figured even just a few days in London might help. Dinner with his parents and shuffling around his own house —a house that had felt too big and empty for years. It was home. Sort of. He'd been in England long enough that it felt like a place he belonged. And Shane had never been there with him. No painful memories lingered in those walls. Maybe that would be enough.

Jesse didn't know *what* would be enough in the long run if Shane never came back. Nothing had really made him happy. Sure, he'd felt good when his band gained fans and recognition, sure it was gratifying to know he could help his parents and they didn't have to worry about retirement. But it wasn't enough. And he kind of hated himself for that. He didn't *want* to miss Shane anymore. He wanted to have him. Or walk away.

Dinner with his parents did help. His mother was sweet and concerned. As usual. She'd been concerned the entire summer, checking on him daily to see how he was handling being with Shane after all that time. "Mom, I'm a grown man. I'm fine," didn't really seem to do much to appease her worrying.

"How are you, darling?" she asked as soon as he walked in the door. His parents' beautifully and expensively decorated Notting Hill townhouse was everything his mother had ever wanted. No part of it resembled the simple house he grew up in. Jesse was happy he could buy it for them, but it didn't feel like home.

"I'm fine, Mom." Same as always. Fine.

"No, you're not. Did Shane do something to you?"

Jesse groaned. "Why do you always assume it's about Shane?"

"Because it always is."

He shook his head and hugged his mother, gave his dad a quick hug and a pat on the back, then slid into his usual spot at their table.

"How long are you here?" she asked.

"Just a few days. We're playing Madison Square Garden on Friday."

His mother used to track all of his show dates, the cities he was in, the television appearances. He'd told her to stop a long time ago. It was too much, and she worried constantly. A call or a text was usually enough for her these days. But she reminded him all the time that he was still her baby.

"Are you enjoying this tour?"

Yes. No. All of the above. "Shane figured out it was me. I, well, I sort of told him."

His mom shook her head. "I don't know how he missed it, darling. That boy loved you, and looks aside, you haven't changed a bit."

Jesse shrugged. "I have, kind of. When I'm being Kayden I'm different."

"You're still my little boy."

He smiled. "You always say that."

"It'll always be true. Did he take it well?"

"Not really." Understatement of the millennium.

"Are you two giving it another shot?" His mother had always been able to read him, but this was like telepathy or something. How had she known? He'd had nothing but bad things to say about Shane for years.

"It's not like that, Mom."

"I'm not blind, dear. I never was."

Jesse sighed. "Okay, I don't think it's like that. I'd... I'd like it to be, though. I don't know if it'll happen. He's angry."

"Just give him time. He still loves you as much as you love him."

Time.... Jesse had time to give. And he was willing to wait it out if that's what it took. *If* at the end of the wait, he had Shane again. That was a pretty big *if*. He gritted his teeth and tried not to think about it.

CHAPTER TWELVE

Shane entered Madison Square Garden with nervousness fluttering in his belly. He timed his arrival so Moonlight would already be onstage. It had been decided that for the latter portion of the tour, Moonlight would perform first, the opposite of the arrangement they had for the overseas leg. Shane was grateful for the switch. He wanted his presence to be a surprise to Jesse.

Nick already knew he was coming. They'd met up a few days before, had a talk. Em and the other members of the band had been given a highly edited version of what had happened and why Shane left. They were all still mad at him. Shane couldn't say he blamed them. He let his emotions get the better of him and nearly caused irreparable damage to the band and their reputation. As it was, they were planning a couple of free concerts at the venues he'd missed to make it up to the fans.

For violating his contract, he was going to have to pay Blue Horizon a fine, which he'd been told would cover the loss of profits to the label for the apology concerts after the tour. All things considered, it was a slap on the wrist, and he counted himself lucky.

Shane stopped in the greenroom to briefly greet his bandmates and then made his way up to the stage with his acoustic. He stayed in the wings, close enough to see what was happening without being visible himself. Jesse stood in front of the microphone in full-out Kayden mode, glittery blue guitar and all.

He wore a pale pink T-shirt and pants cut so low the tops of his hip bones were exposed. He was beautiful, as he'd always been, but more so because Shane finally understood the draw, the pull he felt toward Kayden since the very beginning. He was Jesse, the one and only person Shane had ever loved, other than his brother Nicky. The one he'd never been able to forget. For that reason alone, Shane was willing to forgive him.

It took him a couple of days to reach that conclusion and the rest of the week to decide just what he was going to do about it. Jesse had done what Shane hadn't been able to bring himself to do. He came to Shane and admitted he'd been wrong. He bared his soul, and Shane had let him leave without even accepting his apology. Shane had his excuses, and he needed the time. But he knew he had to make it up to Jesse, and he'd found the perfect way to do it.

He finished their song—the one they started in Jesse's bedroom all those years ago, the one Jesse had used to hurt him. But he altered it so it matched up to their original intentions that day. "Second Glances" was finally as it had been meant to be—a song about love, about finding the person you couldn't live without and never letting go.

According to Moonlight's normal set list, Jesse's most famous piano ballad, "Epitaph," was only a couple of songs away. Shane's plan was to go out onstage after "Black

Heart," which immediately preceded the ballad, and ask Jesse to sing "Second Glances" with him instead. It would be their first duet.

Anxiety built in Shane as the song Jesse was singing ended and they started the next. Only his brother knew what he planned to do. When Shane told him, Nick just shook his head and made a snarky comment about being glad he was still in possession of *his* balls. Typical Nicky. Shane took it in stride. After all these years, it was hard to be offended. He knew Nick didn't seriously mean about ninety percent of the shit that came out of his mouth.

"Black Heart" drew to a close, and Shane sucked in a deep breath. There was always a slight delay as Jesse switched from the guitar over to the concert grand. Shane stepped out onto the stage in the midst of the audience's applause. The energy from the fans instantly changed. The clapping grew more frenzied; screams and cheers rang out. They probably hadn't expected he would be there after missing the previous two concerts.

Shane waved to the crowd with one hand. In the other he clutched the neck of his six-string acoustic. Jesse had been facing the opposite direction, heading toward the gleaming piano in the center of the stage, when Shane stepped out of the wings. Shane saw him slow as he sensed the sudden shift from the audience. Jesse glanced over his shoulder, saw Shane, and froze midstep.

He didn't move until Shane was standing right in front of him; then his face lit up and that gorgeous smile curved his lips. "You came."

Shane nodded, trying to keep his face serious so his nerves didn't show. "There's a song I want to sing with you. How about we skip 'Epitaph' tonight?"

Jesse looked a little confused, but he answered gamely. "Sure."

Shane grabbed Jesse's hand and tugged him back to the main microphone. The crowd had grown quiet enough that the rapid thud of his pulse seemed loud in his ears. He didn't know why he was so nervous. He was used to performing to thousands of fans in packed arenas, but he'd never sung a duet with Jesse, not even when they were in Luck together. He'd done backup vocals then, but that wasn't the same. That was supporting Jesse, not being center stage with him, and Jesse was undoubtedly the better singer. Shane tried to shake the feeling off. It didn't matter who was better. All that mattered was the song. And Jesse, whose hand felt so absolutely right in his, it almost hurt to think about letting go.

"Hello, all," Shane said into the mic. "This song is the first collaboration between Moonlight and Luck. It's called 'Second Glances.'" He looked sideways at Jesse, who appeared even more confused than he had before. "We hope you like it."

Shane released Jesse's hand with reluctance. He strapped on his guitar, adjusted it, and began the familiar chords and strumming pattern. Jesse looked uncertain, but he started singing almost automatically when he heard his cue. Shane gave him an encouraging smile and joined in:

"Second glances,

warmed from the sun,

moments slow passing,

never done."

Shane felt a chill trace down his spine, the way it had the first time he heard Jesse sing those lines. Their voices entwined, Jesse's rich, throaty tenor and Shane's smoky baritone.

"For the first time,
someone sees who I am,
and I can't let you
slip through my hands.
So hold me closer,
never push me away...."

Jesse trailed off after that verse, and Shane knew why. That was where Jesse had added the lyrics, the cruel ones, meant to inflict pain. But Shane had his own lyrics. He went on:

"You are my heartbeat,
my soul and my life.
All I ever wanted
was to hold you at night."

Jesse's eyes widened; his lips parted in surprise. Shock and joy mingled on his features as he took in the new words.

"Won't let anger
or my stupid pride
ever keep me from wanting
you by my side...."

He sang the last few lines with Jesse staring at him in wonder. Shane could see that he was trembling and his eyes, sea green because of the contacts, were wet. Jesse blinked hard a couple times, as if trying to keep the tears at bay. The applause from the crowd was deafening, but all of Shane's attention was focused on Jesse's face. Everything else seemed to blur around them and the noise faded to a dull roar.

Shane leaned close, with his eyes locked on Jesse's. He spoke softly under the chaos of screaming and yelling that came from the audience.

"I love you, Jess. Now. Always."

Jesse didn't reply, just reached up to cup Shane's nape

and pull him closer. Their mouths met, and the noise from the crowd vanished. Jesse kissed him with pureness. Tenderness. With heart and soul and quiet passion. Nothing that had come before could compare to it.

Shane knew he would go to his grave with the memory of that kiss on his lips.

When Jesse finally drew back, Shane was completely overwhelmed. He stared down at Jesse, stunned beyond speech. Jesse smiled, slow and tremulous, as if he knew everything Shane was feeling. Because he felt it too.

The fans were going bat-shit. In his periphery, Shane could see them, flailing around, jumping, clapping. But the only thing he heard was Jesse's voice.

"I love you too."

Shane jogged offstage, waving, to the roaring of fans after Luck completed their final encore song. The show had been exhilarating, fun, wonderful... and the longest goddamn hour of his life. After that song with Jesse, after their kiss, all he wanted to do was take Jesse in his arms and disappear for days, weeks, as long as it took them to get back to the place they were at when they were kids and nothing was more important than the way they felt about each other.

Jesse was waiting for him on the side of the stage, smiling like he always used to. Shane couldn't believe he'd been fooled for even one second.

"Hey," he murmured.

Jesse came up and kissed him, sweaty concert face and all. "Hey, yourself," he answered in that voice Shane loved, his accent nearly gone, all Jesse. The contacts were gone too, and those gorgeous gray eyes looked up at him adoringly. Shane knew he looked the same way right back at Jesse. He didn't think he'd ever get used to it.

"Love you, Jess," Shane said.

Once hadn't been nearly enough. He wanted to keep saying the words over and over. They'd been waiting to come out for more than eleven years, after all. Jesse smiled and leaned up to kiss him again.

Dre, who was brushing by them, stopped short. Nick ran into him, followed by Will. Shane had to hold his hand out to keep them from toppling down.

"Wait. Love you? What the hell?" Dre choked out. His caramel skin turned ashen. He gaped at Jesse and Shane, clearly looking for a sign that he hadn't heard what he thought he just heard.

"I thought Shane took off and made us look like assholes because you two were fighting, and now you're all lovey? And since when is Kayden's name *Jess*?"

Shane glanced at Nick. "You didn't tell him?"

Nick shrugged. He looked annoyed. "Not my shit to tell."

Jesse cleared his throat. "It is me, Dre. Jesse." He ran his hand down Shane's arm and twined their fingers together. Dre's mouth opened and closed, fish-like, for a few seconds before he clamped it shut. "I'm sorry. I should've told you."

"*Jesse* Jesse?"

Jesse nodded. "Yep."

"What the... *fuck?*" Dre reached out for support and grabbed one of the beams that crisscrossed along the wall backstage.

Shane chuckled. "That's pretty much the reaction I had."

"And you knew this all along?" He looked at Shane accusingly.

Shane shook his head. "No. Definitely not. Not till Chicago, although I'm not sure how I could've missed it." Every time he looked at Jesse, his face felt more familiar: small and delicate, but still the guy he fell for all those years ago.

"But...." Dre gestured at Shane and Jesse. "Why, how.... Jesus. When the hell did *this* happen?"

Shane smiled. He pulled Jesse's hand up to his mouth. "A long, *long* time ago," he answered.

"And an hour ago," Jesse added.

Shane couldn't help laughing. He was so damn happy it didn't matter if they weren't making sense. Dre looked pissed and confused. "Listen, it's a long story, bro. Jess and I will sit down and tell you another night. Right now, I need to eat and get some shut-eye."

"Whatever. I don't get you, dude. And you...." Dre looked at Jesse and sighed. Then he pushed past them to the stairs that led to the band's changing rooms.

"You think he'll be okay?" Jesse asked.

"Yeah, he'll be fine—and if not? I ruined over ten years of my life for those guys. It's my turn now."

"And mine." Shane couldn't help but smile at the possessive look on Jesse's face.

"I can't keep my hands off you," Shane moaned. He wrapped Jesse in his arms. "So much of me still can't believe this is happening."

"Me neither." He gave Shane a hesitant smile. "You ready to go?"

"Definitely."

JESSE'S HANDS shook a little while he waited for Shane to unlock the door to his sleek, modern condo. The place was a little scary. Being alone—really, *really* alone—with Shane for the first time after everything that had happened between them was a hell of a lot scarier. Shane opened his door, then turned to look at Jesse.

"Hey," he murmured. "You okay?"

"Just nervous, I guess."

Shane chuckled. "It's just me, Jess. Remember all those afternoons we hung out in your room and played music and kissed and stuff. We can be like that again, right?"

"You don't think you made me nervous back then?" Jesse's stomach was weak, but it felt good. Fluttery and wonderful and exactly like he remembered. He hadn't let himself feel it all those long months on the road. Every time the giddy happiness tried to come up, he'd forced it down as hard as he could. It was nice to finally let go.

Shane cupped his face with trembling hands and kissed him slowly. *God,* it was amazing.

"You make me nervous too. And happy, and scared and like I can barely keep from laughing half the time over nothing. I think that's what it's supposed to feel like when you're in love."

Jesse ground his face into Shane's neck and hugged him as tightly as he could. They walked awkwardly into Shane's condo, kissing and holding each other, dropping instruments and duffel bags, pants, shoes, shirts.... By the time they got to Shane's enormous bedroom and the pale-green tiled bathroom beyond, it was just them—sweaty skin, swollen lips, hair crunchy from stage products, eyeliner smeared from half-shed tears.

Jesse reached into the shower to turn it on and was shocked when an icy blast hit his arm. Shane chuckled and twisted the knob until the water was warm, and the room filled with steam.

"C'mon, Jess. I always wanted to do this with you when we were kids."

It was something that Jesse, in his past incarnation, would've never dared to dream of. He and Shane, wet, huddled as close as they could get under the showerhead, and still squeezing tighter together. Warm water rinsed them clean of sweat and grimy makeup. Jesse reached for Shane's shampoo and poured some into his palm. He massaged it into Shane's hair and reveled in the moans and whimpers he got in return.

"Love your hands on me," Shane murmured. "I always have."

"Me too."

Shane smiled and filled his palm with shampoo to return the favor. "You used to be so shy when I wanted to touch you. Like you couldn't believe I really did." Shane's long-fingered hands slid through his hair, lathering gently. Jesse shivered. It felt so perfect. They were finally touching the way it was meant to be. No anger, no resentment, just wonder.

"I guess I *couldn't* believe you really wanted me. I was dorky and chubby and so damn insecure. That's what made it so easy to believe that you were done with me. I didn't even question that you really meant it."

"Oh God, Jess. I *wasn't* done with you. I loved you so much. That day was torture. I fucking cried that night. For hours. I almost called you so many times." Shane's voice cracked.

"Shane, it's over. We're here now." Jesse wiped the shampoo from Shane's forehead and guided him under the water to rinse his hair clean.

"How can you be so wonderful to me? *Fuck.* I took eleven years of our life together away. We could've been like an old married couple by now. You and me always. Like it was supposed to be."

Jesse's chest ached at the thought of the time they could've had. But it was gone, and all that was left was the future. "It can be like that now. I still don't want anybody else. I never did."

"Me neither. None of them. I just want you."

Jesse smiled. "So let's start tonight. We can't pretend those years didn't happen, but they're gone and we're back, right?"

"Yeah." Shane gulped and wrapped his arms tightly around Jesse. "I'm trying to be cool... but I just have these moments where I start fucking panicking."

"About what?" He squeezed Shane back.

"What if you never came to find me? I thought about you all the damn time, about looking for you, trying to apologize, even though I had no idea where to start. I'd have never found you. Not in England. Not with a different name."

Jesse smiled. "Yeah, I was hiding in plain sight, I guess you could say. You knew where I was all along; you just didn't know it was me." He reached up and took Shane's face in his hands, that wonderful, familiar face, older but exactly the same. "Listen, don't worry about it, okay? I was never not going to reach out to you. Sure, I had this whole revenge plan in my head, but I swear most of it was me wanting you back in my life. I just went about it the wrong way."

"I don't care. I have you back. That's all that matters. It was always you, Jess. Always."

"Even when you thought I was someone else?" Jesse teased. He had to tease to cover the thickness in his throat.

"I'm such an asshole," Shane muttered.

"Babe, I was kidding. Come on, let's get out of here. No more beating ourselves up. Time for loving, okay?"

Shane turned off the water and grabbed a towel from the hook on his wall. He dried Jesse off with long, gentle swipes before running it cursorily over his own skin. When he was finished, he pulled open one of the drawers under the sink and withdrew a bottle of lube and some condoms.

"Are we going to need these?" Shane asked. He looked sweet and unsure and so unlike any version of Shane Jesse had ever seen that Jesse had to grin.

Jesse reached out and took the lube from his hand. "We definitely need this," he said. Then he plucked the strip of condoms from Shane's fingers. "And these too. For a while at least."

Shane smiled shakily. "Now I'm nervous."

"No need to be," Jesse lied. His stomach was quaking as well. But someone had to lead the show, or they'd both end up in a shaky ball in each other's arms. "We've done this before, right?"

"But that wasn't *us*. It was... different."

"Well, it's us now. Exactly how it would've been all those years ago. Except I'm not an insecure virgin anymore. And you? You're still every dream I've ever had."

Shane groaned. "I love you so much."

"Come show me." Jesse held out his hand and tried to hide the tremble.

Shane *was* every dream he ever had. Even when those dreams were angry, there was yearning, love, and desperate want threading through them and holding him together. The anger was gone, finally, and all that was left was the love and the yearning. The want had magnified to a need so big he could barely stand it, and Jesse wanted to feel it all.

They sank slowly onto Shane's big, expensive bed. It

was a far cry from the rickety twin Shane had back when they were kids—where they came together on that wonderful night when they'd come so close to where they were about to go. Jesse wanted to feel Shane inside of him. All of Shane, not just his magical fingers. Even that much was so many years ago Jesse didn't know what was real and what was long-held fantasy.

"I want you," he said and pulled Shane close. "Just like it should've been a million years ago."

"You don't want to fuck me again?" Shane asked. "I... I loved it."

Jesse had loved it too, after he let go of his stupid anger and pride. But it wasn't what he needed. "I do want to be inside of you again. Of course. I want *all* of it with you. But tonight? Right now? I need you. Like we always planned."

"O-okay." Shane agreed, but he wasn't sure. He didn't know if he could go through with it, take Jesse like he always used to want to. He wanted to be the possessed, the taken, the one who was surrendering. He needed to show Jesse that this time it was forever.

"Shane, it's okay. I want this. I need to feel like I belong to you again. Those few short months when you and I were together, nothing else in my life has ever felt that real."

"No. Nothing. We do belong to each other. That's why it always felt off when we tried it with someone else."

Jesse smiled, that sweet, gorgeous, not-Kayden-Berlin-at-all smile. Shane's heart thumped. It was like going back in time. He leaned forward and kissed Jesse with his eyes closed, and could swear he smelled his old room — blueberry candles, old socks, and the dusty late summer air. It was summer when he and Jesse fell in love. Maybe it was fate that it happened to be summer when they found each other again.

Jesse spread his perfect thighs and pulled Shane between them. Shane went willingly, leaning on his elbows to kiss and taste. The skin of Jesse's neck was soft and sweet and clean. His lips parted slowly, letting Shane in. It was a new kind of kiss. Not like when they were kids and Jesse was shy, allowing Shane to take control. Not like in Chicago either, when he was dominant and angry. They were equals. Together.

"You feel good," Jesse whispered. He pushed his hips up against Shane's.

"So do you." Shane wanted to tell Jesse he loved him again, that he'd never leave him, but it would be too much, right? Too overwhelming. So he didn't. He just kissed the man he'd barely survived without for way too long and soaked in the feel of his touch.

"I want your fingers in me," Jesse moaned. "You have no idea how long I've been dreaming about it."

"Oh God. That night. I wanted you so bad, Jess." Until the night with Jesse back in Chicago a few weeks ago, it had been the most purely erotic moment of Shane's life.

"I wanted you too." Jesse rolled to his stomach. "Just... now. Please?"

"Yeah. But first... I wanted to do this when we were kids. I just hadn't before and I wasn't sure what to do." Shane leaned over and ran his tongue up the perfect round curve of Jesse's ass. Jesse moaned in anticipation. "You want it?" Shane asked tentatively.

"Are you kidding?" Jesse answered with a quiet choked laugh. He tilted his hips up into Shane's searching touch. "*Yes.*"

Shane leaned over and kissed the crease where Jesse's

ass met the top of his thigh. "So soft." Shane rubbed his lips along Jesse's skin. It felt like velvet, smooth and covered with little tiny hairs that tickled his lips. He bit experimentally on the inside of one of Jesse's cheeks, then separated them and placed a nuzzling kiss right on the entrance to Jesse's body. Jesse moaned and shivered.

"Can't wait to taste you," Shane murmured, almost to himself, then he took one long initial taste, swirling his tongue around Jesse's hole and pushing just a little at the muscles to get them loosened up. Shane trembled at the heat, at the knowledge that it was *Jesse* he had his mouth on. Jesse, who was clean, warm, sexy, and all his.

"Oh *fuck*," Jesse moaned. "That's incredible."

"You want some more?" Shane teased with a smile. All he got in return was a needy little whimper hot enough to almost make him come. He delved back in and tasted some more, licking, kissing, and pulling Jesse's cheeks apart so he could get closer, more, everything he wanted. Jesse was losing control beneath him, writhing, whimpering, trying to get as close to Shane's mouth as he could.

"Shane. Fingers. *Please.* I need it."

Shane choked out a moan and traveled up Jesse's back, dropping kisses and bites all along his spine. His fingers rested where his tongue had been, no pressure unless Jesse wanted it. He did. Jesse pushed back against Shane's fingers hard.

"Inside," he moaned.

"Lemme get some lube, baby. I don't want to hurt you." Shane wanted inside so damn bad, but he had to take it slow, remember every single moment.

"Okay." Jesse smiled. "You called me baby. I missed that so much."

"Me too." Shane clicked open the lube and drizzled it

on his fingers. Then he knelt over Jesse and brought his hand to the entrance of Jesse's body before leaning over to suck at his neck. "So tight," he whispered. "I can't wait to feel you."

Jesse growled. "Inside, Shane. *Now*."

"Like this?" Shane pushed in slowly with two long fingers. *Holy fucking hell.*

Jesse was so tight and hot, and he was going to feel so amazing around Shane's cock. But not yet. Not until he was begging for it. Until then, he would suck on Jesse's neck and listen to those moans and whimpers that were a thousand times better than any porn and, *fuck*, keep his fingers buried deep and rubbing Jesse in all the right places… like riiiight there.

"Holy *Jesus*." Jesse froze. "Stop before I come, babe." Shane didn't listen. He grinned and rubbed at Jesse's prostate again and reveled in low heated screams. "Oh God, stop, *stop*—no, don't stop, that's so fucking good."

Shane added a third finger and let Jesse fuck himself on them until he was shivering and whimpering, flushed and covered in a sheen of sweat.

"You ready for me now?" Shane whispered, bathing Jesse's ear with his breath. Jesse shuddered hard and froze. "Jess?"

"*Wait*… trying not to come." He stayed there, still for a good thirty seconds. "Okay. I'm good."

Shane slid his fingers out and let Jesse fall onto his back. "Why didn't you let it go, baby? I would've have liked the challenge of making you come again." He grinned down at Jesse and leaned over to kiss him.

"I just wanted you to be in me when it happened." Jesse reached above his head to the nightstand where the condoms were. He ripped one off and tore it open. Shane went to take the condom, but Jesse held it. "Let me put it on you."

It took a lot of jaw clenching and raw willpower to stay still while Jesse slowly rolled the latex down his super-sensitive length. It took even more to watch Jesse drizzle lube on his cock and rub it in with this sexy-as-hell, naughty smile on his face.

"Come here and fuck me," he finally said. "I've been waiting for this moment for way too long."

Shane slung one of Jesse's legs over his elbow and leaned closer. "Me too, Jess. I've been waiting forever. I love you."

"Love you too—" Jesse gasped and arched his back as Shane sank into him. "*Yes*," he hissed. He dug his free heel into the bed and lifted into Shane's stroke.

Shane let Jesse's leg slide off his arm so he could put his elbows on the bed by Jesse's face and kiss him. No matter how amazing the rest of it felt, kissing was by far the best. Jesse's seeking tongue, the taste of him, the way he breathed hard on Shane's mouth. It was so perfect.

"I don't know how I lived without you," he murmured.

"Barely," Jesse sighed in return. "Me too. I'm so yours. Oh fuck, Shane, right there. *Ohh*."

Jesse convulsed and tightened on his cock. Shane sat back onto his heels and spread his own legs so Jesse's thighs were splayed wide over his, leaving Jesse's dripping cock right there for Shane to play with.

"You're so fucking sexy," Shane moaned. He ran his hand up the middle of Jesse's body—caressing his cock, his chest, lingering a moment at his neck before returning to feel the thump of his heart. Jesse covered Shane's hand with his own and threaded their fingers together. He undulated on the bed, forcing Shane's dick as deep as it could go.

"Love this. Love you." Jesse's voice trembled. He pulled Shane's hand to his mouth and kissed his palm. They smiled at each other then, small intimate smiles that said everything they had yet to say.

We're in this forever, Jess. You and me.

Shane dragged his hand back down Jesse's chest and wrapped it around Jesse's throbbing cock. He started stroking, pulling in time with the rhythm of his hips, aiming for Jesse's prostate with his cock. He wanted to watch his Jess fall apart.

"Shane, I'm gonna come." Jesse sounded panicked, pleasure-drenched, like he was coming apart at the seams.

"I want you to come, baby. I wanna see it. Let it go."

Jesse froze and then came with a wail, squeezing Shane's cock and splattering his chest with release. "O-oohh."

Shane watched in awe, trying to hold himself back. Then Jesse squeezed his cock one more time and it was too late. He lost it in the heat of Jesse's body until he was trembling and still and slumped over just a little. Jesse sat up and ran a hand up Shane's body until his arm curled around Shane's neck and they were kissing. Their bodies were still connected. Shane didn't want it to end.

"It was better," Jesse whispered between kisses.

"Hmm?"

"I've been imagining it for years, what it would be like between us if we were together again for real. It was so much better." Jesse's voice sounded thick, like it was hard to push the words out.

All Shane could do was nod because there really were no words.

It was perfect.

EPILOGUE

"Hmm... something's not quite right yet. Play it one more time."

Shane nodded and replayed the chords that Jesse had asked for, picking at the strings of his acoustic guitar with the type of easy skill born from years of practice. They'd been lounging in the living room of his condo all afternoon, working on one of the tracks for their upcoming acoustic album. An array of snacks was spread out on the coffee table between them. After several run-throughs, he knew the chords so well he could've probably played them in his sleep. So instead of focusing on the guitar, he watched Jesse's face as Jesse watched him.

Jesse was on the couch across from him, sitting with his back to the floor-to-ceiling windows that overlooked the city. Much like when they were kids, he sat cross-legged with a notebook resting on his knee. As he listened, he chewed thoughtfully on his lower lip, his head held cocked to the side, and toyed idly with the pen he was using to take notes.

The pose was so familiar that Shane couldn't help but grin. Sometimes he still had a hard time believing Jesse had managed to fool him all those months they were on tour. Perception was a funny thing. He'd never expected to see Jesse again. Even though, looking back now, Shane could easily see all of the clues he somehow missed when he and Kayden first met—the mannerisms, that smile, the voice that to this day gave him chills—at the time he'd been so totally fucking oblivious. It almost made him wish he could go back and slap himself. How could he not have realized? In hindsight it seemed so very obvious.

Aside from Jesse and Kayden, no one else had ever stirred any *real* interest in him. That in itself should've been his biggest clue. But even despite the fact that Kayden's true identity had come as such a shock during that concert back in Chicago, Shane was pretty sure on some deeper, basic level, his heart had always known.

"Maybe we should repeat it a fourth time," Jesse said when Shane finished playing. He set his notebook aside and reached for his own guitar. "And then maybe if we switch up the bridge a little bit...."

Shane's grin widened as Jesse strummed a few chords and then paused to scribble something in his notebook, furrowing his eyebrows in concentration. Sometimes there were these little moments that took him back to when they were kids and spent countless hours locked away in Jesse's room, just talking and playing and listening to music.

Shane could almost see a teenage Jesse in his head, doing that same exact thing and wearing that same exact expression, except with his glasses perched low on the bridge of his nose. Now that Jesse looked so different, the memory was kind of bittersweet.

Jesse wasn't wearing his contacts, which these days he only used to change his eye color anyway. Instead of being sea green, his eyes were back to that gorgeous steel gray color Shane had always loved. His hair was still Kayden's icy blond, and while Shane liked it, he did wonder how Jesse had put up with maintaining it for so long. For Shane, the constant trips to the stylist would've gotten old *really* quick. But then, he never spent all that much time on his own personal appearance. Outside of his normal shave and shower routine, his only real concession to vanity was the occasional application of eyeliner and the rare Dior shopping spree.

Not that he'd ever complain about Jesse's new routine. The blond was nice, even if he did prefer Jesse with darker hair, but it wasn't the hair on his head that mattered to Shane—it was the lack of it everywhere else. Jesse kept his entire body free of hair and silky smooth. In the past Shane hadn't cared about that kind of thing one way or the other, but with Jesse just the idea of all that sleek, bare skin sent a shiver of heat straight to his groin.

Shane set his own guitar aside and leaned back against the couch, trying to ignore the telltale bulge in his jeans. God, how was it possible that after three months of nearly constant sex he still wanted Jesse so badly?

They'd been off tour for a few weeks, and barring a short trip to London for Jesse to collect some more of his belongings, they hadn't been apart since. If it were up to Shane, they never would again. He loved having Jesse with him all the time, falling asleep together, playing music, making love. The last leg of the tour, after that concert at Madison Square Garden, had been like a fantasy. Part of him still expected that any second he'd wake up and it would've all been a dream.

He wanted Jesse with him every minute of every day. Shane knew that was unrealistic—there would be times when Moonlight was busy in the studio or touring overseas

—but as long as he knew Jesse was coming home to him after, he could deal with those separations. And when he himself wasn't busy with Luck, well, that was simple. Wherever Jesse went, Shane would follow. For the rest of his life he would follow, because now that he had Jesse back, there was no way in hell he was ever letting go.

"I think I've got it." Jesse's face lit up with that sweet, familiar smile. Shane's chest almost ached at the sight of it. *Goddamn.* Even though he was lucky enough to have that same smile bestowed on him multiple times a day, it still had the power to take his breath away. "Listen to this."

Jesse started playing again, but Shane had stopped listening to the music. All he could see was Jesse's face: that dazzling smile; pale, flawless skin; those gorgeous, dark-lashed eyes. There was nothing that wasn't beautiful about him. When they were kids, Shane hadn't seen it right away. That slow-blooming attraction snuck up on him, in little stomach flips and lightning-quick moments when Jesse's smile or his eyes or his laugh made Shane's heart stutter. Until one day he realized that suddenly everything about Jesse turned him on, that somewhere along the way, without ever intending it, he'd fallen for his best friend—*hard.*

Shane couldn't deny his body's immediate response to Jesse's new look, that instantaneous spark of lust that had driven him crazy all spring and summer. He was only human—a fact made painfully clear by his fuckups over the years—and Jesse's Kayden incarnation was sexy as hell. But even back then, when Jesse was more nerdy than chic, when he still wore glasses, when his body wasn't tight and lean as it was now, Shane wanted him. Desperately. More than anyone or anything. He'd wanted to be Jesse's first, his last, his everything. He still did.

"Marry me."

The words were out before Shane could stop them. Jesse's playing broke off in a discordant jangle of notes. He stared at Shane in wide-eyed shock. "What?"

Shane felt heat creep up the back of his neck. He hadn't meant to just blurt it out like that. For weeks he'd been thinking about it, trying to come up with the perfect proposal: where to do it, when, whether or not he should invite Jesse's family to come and be there for the surprise. All that time he'd spent mulling it over and tossing around ideas, only to ruin any kind of grandiose plans by bursting out with it completely at random. And now he couldn't read any reaction on Jesse's face aside from the shock.

Shane sat up straighter and cleared his throat. It wasn't the way he intended to ask, but the words were already out there, and it wasn't as if he could take them back. Not that he actually wanted to.

"Sorry, Jess," he said sheepishly. "I wasn't planning on just saying it like that, but I've been thinking about it for a while now. It's like I told you before, it was always you. For a little while I thought you were someone else, and I'm sorry for that. I don't know how I could've missed it." Shane paused for a second and swallowed thickly. "But you have to know there's never been anyone else. Even when you were pretending, even when I didn't have the first fucking clue, it was always, *always* you. I'll never want anyone but you. I'll never *love* anyone but you. This is forever. You and me."

Jesse was quiet for a long time. He stared at Shane in silence, his expression giving nothing away. Shane stared back, trying to fight off the nerves that were wrecking his stomach. He clenched his hands into fists at his sides to keep them from shaking, but his pulse raced erratically and his heart battered painfully against his ribcage. Finally he managed to swallow and forced two words past his suddenly dry lips. "Say something."

Jesse blinked and dropped his gaze. He sat there for a moment with his eyes fixed on the notebook at his side. Then he put down his guitar and got to his feet.

Shane barely breathed as he watched Jesse round the coffee table. A mix of dread and anticipation twisted his belly into knots. Jesse paused for a second to move Shane's guitar from where it rested on the couch to the floor, and then sank down into Shane's lap without saying a word. Shane instinctively gripped his hips and pulled him closer, but before he could say anything, Jesse's mouth was on his.

"I love you," Jesse whispered. He trailed his tongue teasingly over the curve of Shane's lower lip.

"Jess," Shane started, but Jesse didn't seem to be in the mood for conversation. He deepened the kiss, gliding his tongue over Shane's, and while a distant part of Shane was aware that Jesse hadn't actually answered his question yet, he couldn't bring himself to stop. He moaned quietly and returned the kiss, sliding his hands up Jesse's back, over the buttery soft material of his T-shirt, to grip Jesse's hair.

Jesse whimpered. Shane could feel Jesse's cock, already hard and full, pressing against his own through the material of his jeans. He kept his hands in Jesse's hair and arched up, needing contact, craving friction. After long, breathless moments, Jesse broke the kiss, but he didn't pull away. He pressed down hard against Shane, picking up speed as he moved.

Shane shuddered as Jesse's teeth sank into his lower lip. He moaned and gripped Jesse's hips even tighter, relishing the brief twinge of pain. God, he loved it when Jesse got aggressive like that.

Jesse released the bite and threaded his fingers into Shane's hair, jerking his head back. "Yes," he said.

Shane stared up at him in a daze, helpless to prevent the motion of his hips as he ground himself against Jesse. Damn right yes. It always felt so fucking good.

"Yes, I'll marry you."

Shane froze as the words finally penetrated his lust haze. Then he laughed softly and kissed Jesse again. "Yeah? You're willing to put up with me until I'm gray and wrinkly and maybe can't even get it up anymore?"

Jesse grinned at him and trailed his fingers down Shane's cheek to his kiss-swollen mouth. He rocked his hips, rubbing their cocks together and proving that for now at least getting it up wouldn't be a problem.

"Yeah," Jesse whispered. "And for even longer than that."

ABOUT M.J. O'SHEA

MJ O'Shea has never met a music festival, paintbrush, or flower crown she can stay away from. She loves rainstorms and a perfect cup of tea, beach days, music, bright colors, and more than anything a cozy evening with a really great book.

She is from the Pacific Northwest. While she still lives there and loves it, MJ has the heart of a wanderer. So she puts all her dreams of far off places and extraordinary people in her books.

Except for every once in a while when she does what all travelers have to do on occasion… come home.

ABOUT PIPER VAUGHN

Piper Vaughn is a Latinx author and longtime romance reader. Since writing their first love story at age eleven, they've known writing in some form was exactly what they wanted to do. A reader to the core, Piper loves nothing more than getting lost in a great book.

Piper grew up in a diverse neighborhood in Chicago and loves putting faces and characters of every ethnicity in their stories, making their fictional worlds as colorful as the real one. Above all, Piper believes there's no one way to have an HEA, and every person deserves to see themselves reflected on the page.

Hi Everyone:)

Thanks for getting to know Shane and Jesse — and hopefully falling in love with them like we did. They might not
be perfect, but they're definitely hard to resist.

Also hard for us to resist... Nick. He was trouble, but we
knew when we were writing this that Nick needed his own
story. He definitely got one!

Nick's book, The Luckiest, follows him on his journey to
love and redemption. There's a sneak peek of it coming up
on the next page.

We both love to talk to readers on social media. Please come
find us if you have questions or comments, or you just want
to talk about music:)

xoxo

MJ & Piper

SNEAK PEAK OF THE LUCKIEST

LUCKY MOON BOOK TWO

Beep... b-beep... b-beep....

What the fuck? Nick struggled to open his eyes, but they were heavy, the lids felt glued together, and, *Jesus*, did his head hurt. He couldn't remember what he'd done the night before, but it better have been fucking fun, because he felt like death.

Nick tried to fling his arm out so he could grab whoever the fuck's phone was ringing and smash it against the wall until it shut the hell up. That damn beeping was drilling into his skull. He lifted his arm... but it went nowhere, and a sharp, stabbing pain slammed through his forearm. Tears welled unchecked in his eyes. *Motherfucker.*

He sat up and wrenched his eyes open. Fuck the pain. Fuck it all. But instead of the dark gray walls of his bedroom, he saw blurry, white, institutional-looking walls.

What the...?

Nick focused on the noise. Everything would be okay if only that damn beeping would *stop*. He squinted through his blurry vision, trying to find its source, and realized the sound was coming from a monitor connected to his right hand. His left hand and forearm were covered with a thick cast.

How the hell did he end up in... the hospital? *Oh, hell no. This is* not *happening.* Nick went to wrench the tubes from his arm, but a pair of iron-strong hands pressed him back against the mattress. He tried to fight, but he couldn't sit up. All he wanted to do was fucking sit *up.*

"Nicky, stop. It's Shane. You'll hurt yourself."

Shane?

"Wha—" He tried to speak, but his choked, dry voice made it nearly impossible to push even that one sound from his mouth.

"Here, Nicky. Water." His brother jammed a straw into his mouth, and he took a grateful pull. The water was freezing as it slid down his throat, but it felt pretty damn good.

"Shaney, what am I doing here?"

Nick shifted on the bed. *Fuck.* Even moving a few inches hurt. His head was foggy, his body sore. His skin felt like it had been dragged over a cheese grater at least two or three times. Whatever it was he'd done, that shit couldn't have been good.

"Don't you remember?" Shane's face was annoyed, worried. Scared. Nick knew that look. He'd seen it a million times when they were kids, when they weren't sure if they'd make it out of their dad's house alive. He tried to fight through the painkiller-induced haze.

"Not really. I remember being in the Viper with Dre. It was pretty icy."

"You were pretty fucked-up is more like it. You ran into the fucking window at Saks, Nicky."

Nick squeezed his eyes shut and summoned the pictures he'd thought were a dream—crashing glass, skidding, his arm crunching nauseatingly against the door. He tried to lift his left arm but couldn't... because of the cast. *Jesus*. He'd really done it.

"It's broken. You have cuts all over your body. You've been out for nearly two days. I was so fucking scared, dude."

"Dre?"

"He's banged up, but he'll be okay. You came out with the worst of it."

"Good. When can I get outta here?" Nick made to sit up again, and Shane pushed him down. Again.

"You can't. You're here until your court date. I've been talking to the lawyers for you."

"Court? Can't they just... you know?" Nick waved his right hand. *Make it all go away....*

"No, they can't just 'you know.' Shit, bro. You were caught in a sports car that's barely street legal, high as a fucking kite, with *motherfucking coke* in your pocket. The car was rammed most of the way through the window of a Fifth Avenue store. You could've *killed* someone. The suits at the label are pissed. The boys in the band are pissed. *I'm* pissed. This shit has to stop."

"Hey, at least Em's not pissed," Nick tried to joke. Maybe if he made Shane smile, everything wouldn't seem so shitty.

Shane glared. "*Em* is about to have a coronary. You know he thinks of us as family." Their manager had always treated them like brothers rather than as a means to a buck.

"Well, you can tell him I'm fine." Guess smiling was out of the question.

"They're going to send you somewhere, Nicky. The lawyers think they can cut a deal for rehab instead of jail."

Nick did sit up at that. He ignored his screaming, cut-up skin and the pain in his arm. "Rehab? I'm not a fucking addict."

"You wanna go to jail? I don't think they'd pull a ten-hour celebrity special for this one. You really screwed up."

"I'll pay a fine." This kind of shit didn't *happen* to people like him.

Shane sighed and sank into the plastic-cushioned chair that had been jammed into the corner of the room. "You need help... and I don't think I can give it to you."

"What I need are some better painkillers. You think they have something stronger in this joint?"

Before he turned away, Nick saw Shane slowly shake his head. Damn. He was fucked.

Nick stared at the old brick building through the town car's tinted windows as his driver pulled to a stop. Aside from the address and the word GLENWOOD spelled out in plain white letters above the double doors, the building wasn't any different from the dozen or so others they'd passed on the hospital campus. Depressing. Ugly as hell too. But even with the shit-colored bricks and the bare, creeping vines of ivy that covered the entire right side and part of the front, it didn't look particularly scary.

And yet something about the old place made him feel kind of queasy.

His palms were damp, and he had that churning thing going on in his stomach, like when he'd gotten on the Gravitron at a carnival when he was fourteen after eating too many hot dogs and scarfing down way too much cotton candy. The dizziness was back again, but this time instead of the ride, it was as if the interior of the car itself was spinning and the floorboard under his feet was dropping away. Nausea rolled over him in a wave, and the upchuck rose fast in his throat. Nick did his best to hold it in so he didn't spew all over the snow-covered lawn the moment he got outside, but the effort made his mouth tremble and a sheen of sweat break out on his skin.

Glenwood didn't look like a prison... much. But for all intents and purposes, that's exactly what it was to him. As it stood, he might as well be in for life. Three months was fucking *eternity*, and Nick was there on court-ordered lockdown for exactly that long. He couldn't just walk out if the place pissed him off. He'd be stuck with no car, no license, and no cell phone, so he couldn't even call someone to come get him. Nick had never been so closed off from everything and everyone he'd ever known. Even though he didn't particularly want to see his brother's stupid face ever again, it sort of pissed him off that if he *had* wanted to see Shane, he wouldn't be able to until his counselors gave the okay. Hell, he wasn't even allowed to bring anything in with him except for the clothes on his back. He'd been told everything he'd need would be "provided by the facility."

Fucking rehab. Nick felt like such an asshole. He didn't need some lame-ass, twelve-step program. He wasn't a goddamn junkie. So he liked to drink, and maybe there were times when he needed some smoke so he could chill. And *maybe* he occasionally liked to do a little blow just for shits and giggles. That shouldn't have been a fucking shock to anyone. It wasn't really that big of a deal as far as he was concerned. For shit's sake, it wasn't as if he was some tweaker hanging out on the street corner, offering to suck some guy's dick for another hit of meth.

But his choice was either submit to rehab or risk the chance of jail time, and there was no way in hell he was going to prison to be some beefed-up convict's unwilling bitch boy for however the fuck long they left him there. He wasn't stupid. With a face like his, he wouldn't last five minutes in prison without being bent over the nearest object and ass raped, and then he'd probably get shanked trying to fight the guy off. He'd take rehab over that any day. But fuck if he was going to like it.

The motion of his car door being opened startled Nick out of his thoughts. He went to hide his face, but nothing waited for him on the other side except his driver, a cracked cement walkway, and the ugly-ass building. He took a slow look around but didn't see anything suspicious. They'd circled the area for a long time, trying to lose the reporters who'd been waiting for him outside his condo. He wasn't about to make a damn statement, and he sure as fuck didn't want his picture taken by a flash mob of paparazzi that happened to appear out of the blue as he made the walk of shame into the facility. But it looked like the coast was clear. Thank freaking hell.

Nick slowly got out of the car.

"Sir? Are you ready to go inside?"

Hell no. "Whatever."

Not like he had any choice.

"Here are your latest files, hon. We have a few new patients checking in this morning."

Luka looked up from the meal plan he was working on and smiled at the nurse who'd just set a stack of manila folders on the corner of his desk. "Thanks, Mel."

"You're going to like the guy who just came in."

Luka arched an eyebrow. "Yeah? Why do you say that?"

Melody just grinned at him. "Well, he's kind of battered up and scrawny right now, but once he gets some meat on him...." She trailed off with an appreciative sound, much like someone would make when biting into a slice of gooey chocolate cake.

Luka laughed outright. "Hey, now, remember the rules. No fraternizing with the residents."

Melody winked at him. "I'm going to come back and ask how you feel about that rule once you've actually seen him."

Luka laughed again and shook his head. "Look at you, trying to stir up trouble."

"It's what I do." Melody turned and waved as she left his office. "See you at lunch."

Still smiling, Luka went back to his meal plan. After a few minutes, though, curiosity got the better of him, and he reached for the files Mel had dropped off.

The name on the last file caught his attention. Nicolas Ventura. Why did that seem so familiar? And then he got it.

Luka's eyes widened. *No freaking way.* He hurriedly flipped open the file and checked the picture. It *was* him. *The* Nick Ventura, the notorious rock god who'd been all over the headlines a couple of weeks back after crashing his hundred-thousand-dollar sports car through one of the windows at Saks Fifth Avenue in a drunken haze.

"Oh my God."

Glenwood had treated the occasional C-list celebrity, but never anyone of Nick Ventura's caliber. Even Luka, who wasn't a fan of rock by any stretch of the imagination, knew about Nick's band, Luck, and had heard a few of their songs. Luck had been too big for too long to be completely avoided. Not to mention the recent media frenzy surrounding the marriage of Luck's lead singer, Nick's older brother, Shane, to Kayden Berlin, the gorgeous lead singer of Moonlight, the biggest band to come out of the UK since The Beatles. They were *impossible* to miss.

Luka shook his head in disbelief. He would have bet

everything he owned against Nick being assigned to Glenwood. It was one of the better rehab facilities on the East Coast, true, but they weren't what he would call hard-core. There were other facilities that dealt with people who needed serious help, the kind of people who were so high on whatever they'd been shooting up that they didn't even remember driving into a department store. *That* was the type of place he figured someone with Nick Ventura's problems would end up—at least if the courts made the decision.

Apparently not. Luka shrugged. *He must've had an amazing lawyer.*

Nick stared up at him from the grainy photograph taken during the registration process. Surly. Gorgeous. Dark brown hair fell into his eyes, and faded yellow-black bruises marred the left side of his face. His expression was filled with so much animosity it was nearly palpable, even through the picture.

Oh, he's gonna be a handful. Luka could already feel it.

Melody had been right, though. He was too skinny by far. And judging by his pale complexion and the purplish half-moons under his eyes, he probably hadn't slept well in weeks, if not longer.

It was definitely the worst he'd ever looked, and Luka would know. Thanks to his best friend, Jeana, and her love of trashy gossip magazines, he'd seen dozens of pictures of Nick Ventura over the years. In just the last few months, Luka had watched him go from thin but healthy to exhausted and downright bony. Not a look that normally worked for anyone, but with Nick that wasn't really saying much. Even beat-up and underfed, he was still way too hot for his own good.

He really rocked that whole bad-boy persona too. So much attitude, the stretched earlobe, all those tattoos.

Everything about him seemed hard. Except for his mouth, which Luka had always thought was pretty and soft-looking and maybe just a little bit... vulnerable. And his eyes, which were big and blue and gorgeous and now seemed huge in his overly thin face.

Easy to see why Mel thought Luka might like him. Nick wasn't Luka's usual type, not by a long shot—normally he went for the clean-cut, preppy guys—but there was no denying that Nick Ventura had been blessed with some spectacular genes. Both he and his brother, from what Luka remembered seeing in the magazines. Good looks. Talent. It really was sad to see how far he'd fallen. He'd gone from the top of the proverbial pack to publicly disgraced tabloid fodder pretty much overnight.

Quite the bruise to his fragile little rock star ego, I'm sure.

Nick at least had one thing going for him, though. He'd wrecked his car and caused thousands of dollars in property damage, but he was still alive and breathing. He had time to fix things and turn his life around, and that couldn't be said for a lot of the musicians who'd come before him and died in their prime without ever getting help.

Luka hoped, if nothing else, that Nick would put his time at Glenwood to good use and get his life together. He didn't want to see the guy become yet another "lived fast, died young" cautionary tale that wannabe rockers everywhere just ignored anyway. All Nick had to do was take that first and most difficult step. Easier said than done, though, even for the average Joe. And Nick Ventura, well, Luka had a feeling he was just about as far from average as they came.

Ugh. I need a fucking drink. Nick lay on the twin-size bed in his tiny assigned room, staring up at a water stain on one of the grayish acoustic ceiling tiles and listening to the steady hum of the heater. *Or maybe three.* Hell, even just his iPod would be nice. It'd been days since Nick had listened to any real music. Probably the longest he'd ever gone in... well, *ever.*

He was tired, cranky, and his left arm itched like a motherfucker under the thick plaster cast. He would've killed for a wire hanger to unbend so he could get in there and scratch at it. Nothing but plastic hangers in the closet, though, and the constant itchy achiness was driving him nuts. The squeak of shoes on the linoleum floor out in the hallway was driving him nuts too. The rock-hard mattress. The T-shirt and stupid gray sweatpants he'd been given to wear. *Everything* was driving him nuts.

Nick wanted out, and he hadn't even been at Glenwood for an entire day yet. But there was no out. He was going to be staring at these four walls, and that stained ceiling tile, and sleeping on that uncomfortable-ass bed for the next twelve goddamn weeks, and the very idea made him want to fucking puke.

What had he done to deserve this shit? Nobody had gotten killed. He didn't get why the court wouldn't just let him pay for the property damage and be on his merry way. He'd only lost control of the car because the ground was slick. Could've happened to anyone.

Nick *did* feel bad about Dre getting hurt, though. He'd never meant for that to happen. His entire body had turned to ice when he'd woken up in that hospital room and Shane had told him what'd happened. After that he'd remembered everything: the slick, icy road; Dre asking him to pull over; losing control; that horrible, crunching, jarring impact. He probably should've stopped when Dre asked and just let his friend drive. But it was too late to think about what he *should* have done.

And now here you are, stuck in rehab like a punk.

Nick shook his head and gave a humorless laugh. His life had turned into one of those cheesy-ass *Celebrity Rehab* episodes, which of course he never *ever* watched just so he could make fun of the losers on it. Talk about irony. It sounded like the start of a bad joke. Well, if this *was* a joke, he was still waiting for the goddamn punch line.

At least the worst of his withdrawal symptoms had passed. Those first few days in the hospital had been a bitch to get through. The chills, the body aches, the cramping, clawing pain in his stomach. He was still exhausted and irritated, but most of the physical discomfort was gone except for the perpetual ache in his arm, and nothing but time could fix that.

In a way, Nick was glad for the pain. It stopped him from thinking about Shane. About how, when his lawyer suggested plea bargaining for rehab and fines instead of risking a trial by jury, Shane had agreed without even hesitating. About the fight they'd had the day before the accident, when Shane told him he needed to grow up and be more responsible. Stop with the drugs, stop with the drinking.

He'd gone out the next night just to spite Shane and his bullshit spiel about settling down and getting his shit together. What the hell did Shane know anyway? Just because he'd bought a house and willingly shackled himself to a fucking *husband*, it didn't make him some kind of authority on responsibility. Shane was a goddamn hypocrite. Before Jesse had come back into his life, he'd spent the last decade drinking booze, snorting coke, and banging anything with an ass and a cock. Nick had done the same thing, only with a shitload of pussy thrown into the mix too, which was why Shane's new self-righteous attitude made him fucking *sick*.

But he didn't want to think about Shane. And he sure as hell didn't want to think about Jesse. Underneath it all, Mr. Extreme Makeover was still the same pocket-protector geek from high school whose presence had annoyed Nick from the very start. Nick wished they'd never agreed to the Lucky Moon tour. Things had been fine before then. Mostly fine, anyway.

Looking back, Nick could tell Shane had never really seemed very happy. Not that it mattered anymore. Shane had Jesse, and apparently that was all he needed, because he'd sure as hell been doing a good job of ignoring Nick's existence ever since he'd taken Jesse's dick up his ass and turned into the ball-less wonder. Next thing Nick knew, his brother was writing sappy love songs like he was fucking John Mayer or some shit, proposing, getting *married*. Fuck. Just remembering the pathetic, cock-whipped look on Shane's face during the wedding ceremony made Nick want to gag.

Well, Shane and Jesse could go fuck themselves. So could everyone on the staff at Glenwood. And that asshole judge who'd sent him here in the first place. He didn't want to deal with their dumbass therapy. He wanted to light up a joint, down a bottle of Jack, and forget that any of this shit had ever happened.

Too fucking bad. You ain't getting outta here anytime soon, asshole.

And it was his own damn fault.

OTHER BOOKS BY M.J. O'SHEA

Rock Bay
Coming Home
Letting Go
Finding Shelter

Little Magic
A Little Bite of Magic
A Little Taste of Magic

Sizzle in the Kitchen
Chef in the Wild
Chef vs. Chef
Chef on Top

Dangerous Attractions
Grifter's Gambit
Thief's Temptation
Hunter's Hope

OTHER BOOKS BY PIPER VAUGHN

Hat Trick With Avon Gale
Off the Ice
Goalie Interference
Trade Deadline

Portland Pack With Kenzie Cade
Prickly Business
Prickly by Nature

Hard Hats
Wood, Screws & Nails (with Kade Boehme)
Hook, Line & Sinker

Bookmarked (Heartsville)

Love Rising

Wanting

The Working Elf Blues

www.ingramcontent.com/pod-product-compliance
Lightning Source LLC
Chambersburg PA
CBHW071602150726
48000CB00004B/1563